PRAISE FOR
Gigi Shin Is Not a Nerd

"Move over, Baby-Sitters! There's a new club in town."

—*Kirkus*

"Hand this to readers who enjoy the simple camaraderie and entrepreneurship of 'the Baby-Sitters Club' series."

—*SLJ*

"Via emphatically depicted character interactions, Lee (the Mindy Kim series) skillfully handles topics surrounding cooperation, financial anxiety, first crushes, and pursuing one's goals in this sweet and wholesome new series."

—*Publishers Weekly*

ALSO BY LYLA LEE

Gigi Shin Is Not a Nerd

FOR YOUNGER READERS
The Mindy Kim series

Gigi Shin,
Live from Manhattan

LYLA LEE

ALADDIN
New York   Amsterdam/Antwerp   London
Toronto   Sydney/Melbourne   New Delhi

This book is a work of fiction. Any references to historical events, real people, or real places are used fictitiously. Other names, characters, places, and events are products of the author's imagination, and any resemblance to actual events or places or persons, living or dead, is entirely coincidental.

ALADDIN
An imprint of Simon & Schuster Children's Publishing Division
1230 Avenue of the Americas, New York, New York 10020
For more than 100 years, Simon & Schuster has championed authors and the stories they create. By respecting the copyright of an author's intellectual property, you enable Simon & Schuster and the author to continue publishing exceptional books for years to come. We thank you for supporting the author's copyright by purchasing an authorized edition of this book.
No amount of this book may be reproduced or stored in any format, nor may it be uploaded to any website, database, language-learning model, or other repository, retrieval, or artificial intelligence system without express permission. All rights reserved. Inquiries may be directed to Simon & Schuster, 1230 Avenue of the Americas, New York, NY 10020 or permissions@simonandschuster.com.
First Aladdin hardcover edition April 2025
Text © 2025 by Lyla Lee
Jacket illustration © 2025 by Karyn Lee
All rights reserved, including the right of reproduction in whole or in part in any form.
ALADDIN and related logos are registered trademarks of Simon & Schuster, LLC.
For information about special discounts for bulk purchases, please contact Simon & Schuster Special Sales at 1-866-506-1949 or business@simonandschuster.com.
Simon & Schuster strongly believes in freedom of expression and stands against censorship in all its forms. For more information, visit BooksBelong.com.
The Simon & Schuster Speakers Bureau can bring authors to your live event. For more information or to book an event contact the Simon & Schuster Speakers Bureau at 1-866-248-3049 or visit our website at www.simonspeakers.com.
Book design by Irene Vandervoort
The text of this book was set in Tellumo.
Manufactured in the United States of America 0325 BVG
10 9 8 7 6 5 4 3 2 1
Library of Congress Cataloging-in-Publication Data
Names: Lee, Lyla, author.
Title: Gigi Shin, live from Manhattan / by Lyla Lee.
Description: First Aladdin hardcover edition. | New York : Aladdin, 2025. | Series: Gigi Shin ; 2 | Audience term: Preteens | Summary: "Follows Gigi and her friends to New York City as they attend the art camp of their dreams"—Provided by publisher.
Identifiers: LCCN 2024029274 (print) | LCCN 2024029275 (ebook) | ISBN 9781665939201 (hardcover) | ISBN 9781665939225 (ebook)
Subjects: CYAC: Camps—Fiction. | Art—Fiction. | Friendship—Fiction. | Korean Americans—Fiction. | New York (N.Y.)—Fiction.
Classification: LCC PZ7.1.L419 Gj 2025 (print) | LCC PZ7.1.L419 (ebook) | DDC [Fic]—dc23
LC record available at https://lccn.loc.gov/2024029274
LC ebook record available at https://lccn.loc.gov/2024029275

To all the dreamers and friends out there who make the world a better and brighter place

One

I've always loved summer, but I could already tell this year's was going to be more awesome than the others. After spending almost every weekday afternoon since October tutoring kids with my friends on the Ace Squad, my friends and I had finally raised enough money to go to Starscape, the summer art camp of our dreams.

Everything was coming together!

LYLA LEE

Even though we technically didn't have to keep teaching kids after we made the payment deadline, we didn't want to leave anyone hanging. Plus, Starscape was in NYC, so we were going to need *a lot* more money if we wanted to have fun during our trip. Even after we were all set, my friends and I continued teaching kids in the library. Today I was helping—or trying to help—a fifth grader named Kylie with her homework.

Kylie was new to the Ace Squad, and aside from the few times I'd seen her at my church, I'd never really interacted much with her. All I knew was she always wore black and was super quiet. Even today, when I was trying to guide her through her worksheet about famous American inventors, she barely said anything. Mostly, she just nodded or shook her head.

"Do you remember who invented the telephone?" I asked.

Kylie shook her head.

"I'll give you a hint. There's a type of cracker in his name."

"Alexander Graham Bell?" Kylie asked quietly.

"Yeah!"

Kylie nodded but didn't say anything else.

It was going to be a *long* session.

At the table next to me, my mom flipped through the Korean newspaper. When we first started tutoring, it was just my friends and me and the students. But after our first month, our parents decided we should have an adult chaperone for every session, just in case things got too hectic. And today was Mom's turn. Whenever she was at the library with us, she usually just sat there and read the newspaper. And then, when we finished tutoring, my mom and I dropped my friends off at their houses before heading back home. It was pretty nice.

Toward the end of my session, I got a text from Paul that said, Hey I'm gonna swing by the library later today. Can we meet up after you finish teaching?

Before I could hide my phone, Kylie saw the notification and asked, "Ooh, is that your boyfriend?"

That was the most she'd said all session!

Mom didn't look over our way, but I could tell by her suddenly stiff posture that she was eavesdropping on us.

My heartbeat sped up. I flipped my phone upside down. What could Paul possibly want to meet about *right now*?

"Not really," I said as calmly as I could. "Sorry, let's go back to work."

It took all my willpower to focus on helping Kylie with her worksheet. But even then, I couldn't stop thinking about how Paul and I had been dating for a few months now. I was confused about what was going on between us two, since neither of us had even said the words "boyfriend" and "girlfriend" yet. But today . . . What if *today* was the day Paul wanted to meet up so he could finally ask me to be his girlfriend?

When the session was over and all our students

had gone home, my friends and I regrouped at one of the library tables. Carolina Garcia, Zeina Hassan, Emma Chen, and I didn't all start out as friends, but we were as thick as thieves now. It was one of the best things about being a part of the Ace Squad.

"Hey, did you guys get the welcome packet from Starscape yet?" asked Zeina. "There's a couple of things we have to fill out together, like the roommate selection form."

Carolina groaned. "I still haven't gotten it yet. Or at least, I hope I haven't. Everyone's been so busy after Elisa was born, so it might be in the house somewhere."

Elisa was Carolina's new baby sister. Ever since Elisa was born, Carolina has been coming to school looking disheveled and wearing funny outfits like mismatched shoes and pants that were way too big for her. It made me wonder if things were also this crazy with my little brother Tommy. Since I was only four when he was born, I didn't remember much.

I hoped that, for Carolina, Starscape would be a

nice escape from her chaotic household.

"We should all room together!" I exclaimed. I couldn't imagine going all the way to NYC without staying with my friends.

"Unfortunately, I don't think we can room with more than one person," said Zeina. "The packet we got said each room can only fit two people."

"In that case, how about I room with Emma, and Zeina rooms with Gigi?" Carolina asked. "Since Emma's more my friend than anyone else's. Hopefully our rooms will be close to each other."

"Yeah, hopefully!" Zeina said. "Let's hope we get our picks, period. It says on the bottom of the form that roommate selections aren't guaranteed."

We all groaned.

"You mean we might have to live with total strangers?" Emma complained. "That would really suck."

I bit my lip. Even the slightest possibility that I could be separated from my friends made me anxious. The camp was at NYU this year, which was all over New York City. And NYC was huge! I wasn't sure whether I could navigate all that without my friends.

If only my aunt Yeji replied to my messages, then I'd be able to spend time with someone I know no matter what. My aunt Yeji, or Yeji-imo, as I called her in Korean, was my mom's little sister. She was a super-famous artist who was living my dream life in NYC. She'd left me on "seen" several months ago in October, when I first DMed her that I'd gotten into Starscape. But still, I wanted to meet up with her while I was in town.

She may have been related to my mom, but she and my mom were completely different. I loved Mom, but she wasn't cool like her sister. Even though Mom and Dad were supportive of my art now, they weren't always. And I got the sense that they still didn't truly understand why I wanted to become an artist. I hoped Yeji could at least understand my passion for drawing and making comics. If I could meet up with her, that is.

Maybe she just got busy with all her travels and I would get a reply from her when she returned back home! It seemed unlikely, but I didn't want to completely lose hope.

After we finished our meeting, I got another text from Paul, this time saying that he'd arrived at the library.

I'd been so caught up with everything I had going on with my friends that I'd forgotten to reply to him! In a panic, I grabbed my things as quickly as I could.

"Hey, I have to meet with Paul before we head back home. He just got here," I said, talking to both my mom and my friends. "I'll be back in a few minutes!"

"Ooh, off to kiss your boyfriend?" Emma teased.

Carolina elbowed her.

"Ow!" Emma cried out.

"They're not official yet!" Carolina hissed. "And Gigi's mom is *right* there."

"Oh yeah, my bad!" Emma said apologetically.

We all nervously glanced at Mom, who had her eyebrows raised. I groaned. She and I were probably going to "have a talk" later. Even though, technically,

Paul and I weren't boyfriend/girlfriend. Yet. Although maybe that would all change today.

I could feel everyone's eyes on me as I walked out of the library.

I pulled my shoulders back and took a deep breath. Okay, so I still had to figure out *some things*.

Two

Paul sat at one of the benches by the lake behind the library. He stood up when he saw me exit through the doors.

"Hey," he said. "How was tutoring?"

"Pretty good," I replied. "Sorry I couldn't reply to your texts. I was busy teaching at first, and then my friends and I were talking about Starscape afterward."

"Oh, that's okay. I'm glad I caught you."

Seconds passed. I wanted to ask Paul why he asked to meet up in the first place. His more-serious-than-usual expression told me he had something important to say, although his mouth hadn't said anything yet. Whatever it was, it didn't look like he was about to be sweet and romantic like I'd hoped he would be. I tried my best to hide the disappointment on my face.

My phone buzzed in my pocket. Without even looking, I knew it was either Mom or my friends, probably calling to tell me to hurry so we could all go home.

"Hey, so . . . ," I said at last. "I have to leave soon. My mom is chaperoning today, so everyone is waiting for me since we're their ride back home today. Was there a reason you wanted to meet up with me?"

"Oh!" He frowned. "Sorry. Maybe I should have just waited until tomorrow."

I gave Paul a gritted-teeth smile. "It's okay. What's up?"

He laughed nervously.

"Okay, well, sorry," he said again. "I kind of have bad news. And I figured it's better to tell you this in person ASAP than over text."

My heart dropped to my feet, my thoughts immediately going a million miles a minute.

"What is it?" I asked, already thinking about the worst-case scenario.

"You know how you're going to be in NYC for the first month of summer vacation?"

"Yeah?"

"Well, I just found out that my family is going to Korea this summer. We're going to be gone for pretty much the entire break and will come back the week before the new school year starts."

"Oh." I bit my lip. Even though I was most looking forward to going to Starscape this summer, I'd also been looking forward to hanging out with Paul after I got back. During the school year, Paul was always busy with football practice and other extracurriculars. So summer was supposed to be the perfect time for us to see each other more often. All the cute date ideas I'd saved up in my head burst like popping balloons.

I was disappointed, but I was also glad for Paul. He'd told me how much he missed his family in Korea, since the last time he'd seen them in person was when he was in elementary school.

"I'll have my phone and everything, so we can still FaceTime and stuff! The internet is faster and better there. That's what my mom says anyway," Paul said. "I'm sorry we won't be able to spend time together this summer, though. I don't know about you, but I was looking forward to it."

"Yeah, me too . . ." I trailed off and then shook my head. "But I'm glad you get to go! I remember how much you've been wanting to visit. It's been years, right?"

"Yeah! If my sister weren't graduating from high school this year, my parents wouldn't have planned this trip at all. This is basically her graduation present."

"That's so nice! I hope you and your family have lots of fun."

"Thanks."

We stood there for a moment, staring at each other.

"We still have the rest of the school year," I added. "To spend time together, I mean."

"Definitely. We'll make the most of it!"

I tried my best to smile.

At that moment, one of the doors opened, causing both of us to jump. Emma stuck her head and yelled, "Gigi, let's go! I want to go home. I'm starving!"

"Coming!" I replied, and waved goodbye to Paul.

Paul waved back, watching me go with a nervous grin.

"So, what was all that about?" Zeina asked me when we were all in my mom's minivan.

She and I were seated in the second row, while

Emma and Carolina were behind us in the third. The latest Le Sserafim song came from the very back row, and I knew without having to look that it was Emma listening to her music. She was the biggest K-pop fan out of all of us.

"Paul just wanted to let me know that he and his family are going to Korea for the summer," I replied. "Like, for the *entire break*. They won't be back until a week before school starts again."

"Oh!" Mom exclaimed from the driver's seat. "How fun! I'll have to ask his mom to bring some things back for me if she can."

Most of the time, I forgot Paul's mom and mine were old friends and that our families had known each other since before I can even remember. He and I even went to the same Korean school when we were little kids. Usually, it was too weird to remember all of that history, so I tried my best to not think about it.

"Wait, that sucks!" Emma belatedly exclaimed

as she looked up from her phone. When I didn't respond, she looked from me to the rest of my friends. "Right?"

"Yeah," I said. "I had so many cute summer date ideas planned out for us."

Zeina frowned and patted me on the back. "Sorry, Gigi."

"Well," Carolina said after a while. "At least you'll get to spend plenty of time with us at Starscape! Who needs boys, anyway?"

"Yeah," Emma chimed in. "He's not even your real boyfriend! You should just meet another cute boy in NYC. One who actually *wants* to be boyfriend and girlfriend!"

Both Zeina and Carolina stared at Emma with open mouths.

"Emma!" Carolina hissed. "Cut it out."

My vision became blurry, but I shook my head and faked a yawn, wiping away the sudden rush of tears in the least obvious way I could think of.

"It's okay," I said. "Like you said, I'll have you guys. And my aunt Yeji! If she ever replies to me, I mean."

Out of the corner of my eye, I caught sight of Mom, who was looking at me in the rearview mirror. She didn't say anything out loud, but I could tell from the frown on her face that she was worried about me.

"Yeah, let's make this the best summer possible," Zeina replied, flinging out her arms.

"Yeah!" agreed Carolina.

We all came together into an awkward but fun group hug in the car.

That night I had a nightmare for the first time in a while. My friends were all shouting at each other, our voices so loud that they caused an earthquake. The New York City skyscrapers crashed down around us, and I yelled out, "No!"

I woke up in a cold sweat, my pajamas sticky against my skin.

No way was I letting all that drama happen. Obviously, I knew the falling buildings would never happen, but the fighting . . . things wouldn't really get that bad, right?

It was still dark outside, but I was too lazy to go to the other side of the room and turn the lights on. So, even though I couldn't see anything, I did my best to move around my room. I grabbed my sketchbook from my desk.

And then, hoping it would help me have happier dreams for the rest of the night, I drew a picture of me and my friends peacefully sitting on a bench together in Central Park.

Three

"**Gigi, you're** going to be late for school!"

I bolted up from where I'd been slumped over at my desk. Mom was staring at me from where she stood in the doorway, her mouth wide open in concern. I must have fallen asleep while drawing last night!

"Oh no!" I checked my alarm clock. It was already 8:15 a.m. I only had fifteen minutes to get to school!

I rushed to the bathroom, splashed water on my face, and ran downstairs with my backpack.

"I can drop you off on my way to the store," Mom said. "But I'm about to leave, so hurry!"

My parents owned a small Korean grocery store where a lot of people in our neighborhood went for Korean snacks and cooking supplies. Dad always got up super early in the mornings to open up shop, and Mom usually went back and forth since it was close to our house.

Instead of eating breakfast like I normally did, I grabbed a granola bar and rushed to the garage, where Mom was waiting. She made a disapproving *tsk-tsk* sound as we got into the car.

"You shouldn't stay up so late on school nights," she said. "What are you going to do at Starscape when no one will be there to wake you up for class?"

I groaned. "Hopefully the classes there won't start so early in the day."

"Yes, hopefully! But Gigi, let me know if you end

up getting a tardy slip at school today."

"Will do. Thanks, Umma," I said, saying the Korean word for "mom."

We got to school just as the tardy bell rang, so I didn't have time to check my phone until I'd sat at my usual table with my friends for lunch. But when I did, I got the biggest surprise. There, in my notifications, was a text from Aunt Yeji. I didn't even know she had my number!

Hi, Ji-young, she wrote, using my Korean name. How have you been? Sorry for the super-late response. I was actually in Paris when you messaged me, then it was a busy few months, and I'm finally getting my bearings back in NYC. Your mom gave me your number and reminded me to be in touch. Would totally love to see you when you're in town!! Congratulations on the art program. XO

I screenshotted the conversation and sent it to Mom.

Look! I texted her. Yeji-imo finally replied! We're meeting in NYC!

Let's talk when you get home tonight was all she said in return.

Well, that was rather ominous.

"What's up, Gigi?" asked Zeina.

"Yeah, you've been staring at your phone like it's going to explode for the past five minutes," said Emma, arching her left eyebrow.

"Oh, my aunt Yeji just replied!" I said. "But my mom doesn't seem too happy about it. All she said was that she wants to talk to me after school."

"Weird," Carolina said with a frown. "But wait, isn't Yeji the aunt who left you on 'seen' for months? Are you sure you still want to meet up with her?"

Emma and Zeina also stared at me, looking concerned.

"I mean, yeah!" I said. "She was just really busy. She explained that she didn't get a chance to reply until now because she was in Paris when I messaged her. Isn't that so cool?"

"Paris!" Emma exclaimed. "I love Paris!"

Carolina shrugged. "Well, I'm glad she finally replied!"

"Yeah, me too," I said.

✻ ✻ ✻

When I got home from tutoring, Mom was making dinner in the kitchen. I could tell what today's menu was even without asking because the strong, fragrant smell of kimchi, pork, and onions permeated the house. It was kimchi stew, one of my favorites.

"Hi, Ji-young," Mom said, calling me by my Korean name. "So, Yeji-imo replied to you?"

"Yup!" I said. "She told me to tell her when I'm in town so we can meet up."

"That's great! I messaged her yesterday that you'd be in town, so I was hoping she would reply to you."

With a wooden spoon, she tried some of the soup and then let me try some too. It tasted perfect, so I gave Mom a thumbs-up. She smiled. This was a little ritual we'd been doing whenever she cooked dinner since before I could remember.

"I know you've heard me talk about Yeji-imo already, but I just want to warn you that she is . . . What's the word . . . ? Flaky. She doesn't mean any harm, but she's so busy and disorganized. And she always prioritizes work. She's always been like that."

I frowned. Not sure how to respond, I said, "Oh, okay."

"Just keep that in mind. And don't take it personally if you two don't get to meet up. I really hope you get to see her, though. She *is* very fun. You'll love her."

"I hope so, too!"

First my friends and then my mom. Everyone seemed to believe that I wouldn't be able to meet up with Aunt Yeji. But I still had hope. She seemed perfectly nice over text!

Regardless of whether or not Yeji-imo could actually meet up with me in NYC, I was so happy that everything seemed to be finally coming together. For real, this time. Just a couple of more months of school and then my friends and I would be on our way to Starscape!

four

The next two months whizzed by, and in seemingly no time at all, it was the last day of school.

We had early release today, so when I got home, Mom took me to the mall so we could buy clothes for my trip to NYC. Starscape was only a week away.

Even though my parents didn't say much out loud about Starscape since I'd gotten into the camp, I knew that taking me shopping was Mom's way of showing that she was excited for me. Usually, I got my clothes from our neighborhood thrift shop with my Lunar New Year money, so it was both weird and nice to go shopping with Mom at the mall.

"Are you excited, Gigi?" Mom asked as I was trying on clothes.

"Yeah! If I'm being honest, I'm also a little scared. But I'm mostly excited."

"It's okay to be scared," Mom replied. "It's a completely new experience for you, and it'll be your first time traveling alone, so of course you are. Just know that Dad and I are a phone call away, okay?"

"Okay," I said. "Thank you, Umma. Luckily, I'll have my friends, so I won't be completely alone."

"True! That's definitely a very good thing."

After we finished shopping, Mom picked up Tommy from his friend's house and drove us to Emma's, where my friends and I were hosting an end-of-the-school-year yearbook signing party for all the students and parents we worked with as the Ace Squad.

The moment Mom turned off the engine, Tommy bolted out of the car.

"Bye! See you later!" he said. "I have to start right away if I want to get everyone's signatures!"

"Be careful and don't rush!" Mom yelled after him in Korean as he ran to Emma's front door. But she was smiling, and so was I. Although he was annoying sometimes, it was cute to see how popular Tommy was. It was actually how we were able to get so many elementary school kids to sign up for the Ace Squad in the first place. A lot of our students were his friends.

When Mom and I went inside the house, everyone was sitting either on the sofas or at the kitchen table with yearbooks and Sharpies. It was easy to tell which books were from elementary school and which were from middle school since the elementary school's book was blue, while ours was gold and white.

Tommy was already busily making his rounds to

get his yearbook signed by everyone he knew, while my friends sat around the dining room table. Paul was sitting with the popular kids in the living room. He smiled and waved at me, and I waved back. I definitely wanted to spend some time with him before he left for Korea tomorrow. But I went to where my friends were sitting at the dining room table, first.

Since my friends were artistic and detail-oriented, it was taking super long to sign and draw in everyone's yearbooks. Carolina was drawing Kirby, Zeina's favorite video game character, in her yearbook while Zeina was drawing cute cats and dogs in Carolina's.

Everyone greeted me, and Emma said, "Hey, glad you could make it!" as she handed me her yearbook.

"Hi! Thanks again for hosting this party."

"No problem. Luckily, my parents love hosting parties, so they always like having people over."

She nodded over at the kitchen, where her mom was excitedly chatting with some of the other parents.

"I think she talks to people more than I do," added Emma.

We exchanged a smile and started busily drawing in each other's yearbooks. I already knew exactly what I was going to draw for my friends. Back in the fall, I started drawing a comic about Meteor Girl, a superhero I created. Her friends were all loosely based on my own friends. Emma's character, for example, was named Fashionista, since Emma loved designing her own clothes. So I drew Fashionista on her yearbook.

I couldn't believe how fast this school year had gone by. It seemed like just yesterday my friends and I had created the Ace Squad to raise money for Starscape. And now not only had we met our goal, but we were going to NYC next week. Time went by so quickly!

I was almost done with Emma's yearbook when Mrs. Anderson, Carly's mom, came over to talk to us. Carly was one of our original students. She used to be with me a lot, but since she needed more help with math this semester, she was now usually with Carolina, our main math tutor.

"So, girls, now that you've all raised money for summer camp, what's next for the Ace Squad?" Mrs. Anderson asked. "Are you going to continue the club next school year as well?"

"Yup!" I said. At the same time, Zeina said, "Maybe," Emma said, "Nah," and Carolina said, "We're . . . not sure." We stared at each other. We'd all said different things.

"I might have to focus on school more," Zeina said after a while. She gave us an apologetic smile.

"And I don't know if I'll have time anymore since I'm thinking of joining the robotics club next year," said Carolina.

"I don't have a good reason, honestly," Emma admitted. "I'm just kind of tired of teaching!"

My heart dropped to my feet. Was this really it for the Ace Squad?

This year, Carolina, Zeina, and I were lucky enough to have lunch and art class together, while Emma and the rest of us wouldn't have even gotten close if it weren't for our same lunch period. But next year there was no guarantee that we would have any classes or even lunch together. The only guarantee that I saw my friends every day after school was the Ace Squad. Without the club, what if I never got to see my friends after this year?

Mrs. Anderson laughed nervously. "I guess you girls haven't figured it out yet. Well, let us know if you do! Carly really loves your sessions. You girls helped her out a lot this year!"

"Will do!" I replied, trying to sound cheery.

When the four of us were alone, we stared at one another again.

Before anyone could say anything, I blurted out, "How about we go to Starscape first before we make any hasty decisions?"

I held my breath, afraid that my friends would disagree. But finally Zeina said, "Sounds good!"

Emma nodded while Carolina added, "Yeah, let's take the summer to think on it. Who knows? Maybe things will be less crazy with my schedule by then."

I nodded, deciding to be hopeful. We still had the whole summer. And maybe my friends would change their minds.

There was a tap on my shoulder. It was Paul. I'd been so caught up with club business that I'd forgotten to hang out with him! Luckily, he didn't seem mad or anything. Just kind of nervous.

"H-hey," he said. "Can I talk to you outside for a bit?"

That's odd, I thought. *Why is he acting so weird?*

"Sure!" I replied.

Paul had his shy moments, sure, but he was usually never *this* awkward.

"Ooh," Emma teased. "You guys can go out into my backyard if you want. I wouldn't do anything bad, though, because my mom will probably be watching from the window. Not to be creepy, but to make sure no one gets hurt or does anything they're not supposed to. It's just something she likes to do sometimes."

Paul's face turned bright red. "O-okay."

I smiled, even though I was still dying to know what was going on. He was so cute when he blushed.

Emma's backyard had a comfy white sofa overlooking the pool. It felt like we were at some private resort. Or at least, it was what I imagined a private resort was like. I'd never been to a real one myself, but I'd seen them in the Korean dramas I watched with my mom.

Paul sat down on one end of the sofa and patted the space beside him. He was sitting stiffly, like he was at football boot camp waiting for the coach's instructions.

I looked behind us. Sure enough, like Emma warned she would, Ms. Chang was peering out the window at us, making sure we weren't doing anything weird.

I waved at her, and she waved back.

"Here," Paul said, getting my attention again. He dug into one of his pockets and fished out two bracelets. They were both black, except one had a blue bead in the middle while one had a red one. "I got us matching bracelets. I figured . . . we've been dating for a few months now. And I . . . really like you, Gigi. Sure, we'll always have our phones over the summer, but this way . . . we won't feel so far away from each other. We'll both have these bracelets even when we're on opposite sides of the world."

I looked down at the bracelets and grinned. I took the one with the red bead and shyly peered up at Paul. "Is this you asking me to be your girlfriend?"

Paul slapped his forehead. "Oh right! I was so nervous I forgot to say that part out loud! And it's literally the most important, too. But yeah—yes, I am. If you want to, that is. That's the entire reason I got us matching couple bracelets. Sorry! I can't believe I forgot."

I laughed, and Paul sheepishly grinned.

"It's okay," I replied. "I'd love to be your girlfriend. Thanks so much for getting the bracelets! You're so sweet."

Paul blushed again and said, "Can I put yours on your wrist?"

I nodded happily, and I watched as Paul gently slipped the bracelet around my left wrist and then put the blue one around his.

"Okay, let's go back inside," Paul said. "At this rate, I feel like Emma's mom is going to shoot laser beams at us with her eyes if we stay out here any longer."

He took my hand and got up from the couch. As we walked back inside, I looked down at our joined hands. They looked so cute together, with the matching bracelets around our wrists.

I had no idea what was going to happen this summer, but I was so thankful for this moment. I was always going to remember this day of signing yearbooks with my friends and getting asked to be someone's girlfriend for the first time.

Five

The next week, I met my friends at DFW, which was the airport closest to our town. Since we were too young to fly by ourselves, Ms. Chang, Emma's mom, was coming with us for our trip.

"I'll be staying with Emma's aunt, who lives near Chinatown," she said. "That way I'll be relatively close in case something happens or if you girls need anything."

Even with Ms. Chang there, I was super nervous since it was my first time flying without my family. The only other times I even rode on an airplane were for family funerals in Korea. I was glad today was for a much happier reason, at least.

The airport was full of all kinds of people. Some even wore cowboy hats and boots like people do in the old Western movies.

"You know, I always forget that we live in Texas," Emma said. "But then I come to the airport and see people who still dress like that in real life."

Ms. Chang smiled, and we giggled as we got in line to go through security. Back home, I'd triple-checked my bags in case I somehow accidentally packed something bad. When it was my turn to walk through the scanner, I anxiously watched my bag disappear through the X-ray. Even though I knew I had nothing bad in the bag, I couldn't relax until my bag safely made it to the other side.

"All right, you're good to go," the TSA agent said as I walked through the scanner.

Whew. I was just about to relax when Emma yelled, "Hey, that's my bag!"

Ms. Chang stayed on the other side with Emma while Carolina and Zeina came through and stood next to me. We all gawked as the agent lifted Emma's bag from the scanner and started going through it.

"What did you put in your bag?" Carolina asked. I was wondering the same thing.

"I don't know!" Emma exclaimed. "Nothing that bad, I think?"

At that moment, the TSA agent pulled a bottle of pepper spray from her bag.

"This is definitely not allowed, young lady," the agent said.

Emma slapped her forehead. "Oh yeah, I forgot about that."

Ms. Chang shook her head. "Emma! I thought you said you could handle packing on your own."

"You were going to bring *pepper spray* on our flight?" Zeina asked. "How come?"

Emma shrugged. "We're going to NYC! It might

get dangerous. You never know what'll happen!"

"That is true, but I'm still going to have to take this from you," said the TSA agent, tossing the pepper spray onto the pile of other confiscated items. "Next time put it in your checked luggage. Hope y'all have a good flight."

We stood there for a moment, horrified. But then, slowly, we walked away, laughing as we headed to our gate.

"I can't believe that just happened," I said. "I was so scared we'd be arrested before we could even get on the plane!"

"I was sure they were going to take Emma away from us!" Carolina added.

"Luckily that won't ever happen," Ms. Chang said. "Not on my watch."

We laughed even harder. We weren't even on the plane yet and our trip was already becoming a memorable one.

We'd gotten seats next to each other on the plane, with Zeina and me sitting together in one row and Carolina, Emma, and Ms. Chang sitting beside one another across the aisle from us. It was fun at first, but once we were up in the air, the flight wasn't as exciting as I thought it would be. There wasn't free Wi-Fi, and the movies and TV shows available kind of stank. They didn't even give us meals like they did for international flights.

So all my friends and I did was talk, catching one another up on our lives and plans for the summer as Ms. Chang watched a Chinese drama on her iPad.

"I probably have to stay home the rest of the summer," Carolina said. "The baby is a handful right now. And since I'm the older sister, my parents expect me to help out."

"That sucks," Emma said. "My parents and I are probably going to Paris after we get back from Starscape. My mom promised to take me to a fashion show there."

She tapped Ms. Chang on the shoulder, and her mom took off one of her earbuds. "Yes?"

"We're still going to Paris, right?" Emma asked.

"Definitely!" Ms. Chang said before going back to watching her show.

"That's awesome!" Zeina exclaimed. "Bring us back cool stuff!"

"Already planning on it," Emma replied, giving us a thumbs-up. "I have a list of all the stuff I'm going to get everyone." She looked at both me and Zeina. "What are you two going to be up to?"

"Aya got into Stanford, so we're doing a big family trip to California to help her move in," Zeina replied. "I'm pretty excited!"

"Wow, congrats to her!" Emma said.

"Yeah, that's amazing!" Carolina added. "Stanford is my dream school."

Since the Hassans were our neighbors, my family and I had already congratulated Aya, Zeina's second-oldest sister, on her great news. But I still smiled and said, "Congrats again to her! I hope you guys have fun on the trip."

"Thanks, everyone!" Zeina said. "I'm looking forward to being an only child for the first time in my life."

"It's *amazing*," Carolina said with a groan. "I miss it every day."

"It has its good and bad moments," replied Emma, the only remaining only child out of the four of us. "Mostly good, though."

"That's true," Carolina replied. "I don't miss having one hundred percent of my parents' attention on me. I couldn't get away with anything."

Zeina gulped. "I'm not sure if I'm ready for that."

Emma waggled her eyebrows. "Oh, trust me, there are ways to get away with things. I'll give you some pointers, Zeina."

We all glanced at Ms. Chang, who removed one earbud and said, "Hm?"

We all giggled.

"Thanks, I guess?" Zeina said with a nervous smile.

"What about you, Gigi?" Carolina asked. "What are you doing this summer?"

All my friends turned to stare at me.

I looked around. The only plan I had was the camp, since my parents were usually too busy with the store for our family to go anywhere over the summer. Besides spending time with my family, all I usually did during breaks from school was draw and hang out with friends. I was hoping I could continue tutoring kids through the Ace Squad this summer, but it sounded like everyone else was going to be busy.

"Um, I'm still keeping my options open," I said, my voice coming out higher than normal because of the lie. "One day at a time, you know? I want to enjoy the camp first and figure things out later."

Carolina and Emma nodded, but Zeina gave me a confused look. As my oldest and closest friend, she could always tell right away when I wasn't telling the truth.

Before I knew it, we were almost in NYC. The captain said, "All right, folks, we're going to start our descent into LaGuardia. Please buckle your seat belts if you haven't done so already. Flight attendants, prepare for landing."

"Look!" Zeina whispered, and pointed out the plane window. I followed her gaze to see beautiful, glimmering skyscrapers standing tall against the horizon. Even from this high up, I could see that NYC was way larger than Dallas, the city closest to where we lived. It looked more like Seoul than any city I'd ever seen in the US.

"Wow," I said, my voice coming out hushed like Zeina's.

"We're really here," Zeina said. "We did it, Gigi. In just a few minutes we're going to be in New York City!"

Six

Once we got out of the airport, Ms. Chang called us a taxi.

Our driver drove really fast, yelling and honking at the other cars, pedestrians, and even the pigeons that were flying too close to us. He was exactly like one of those New York cabbies from the movies!

"Whoa," I said as we crossed the bridge into the city. The skyscrapers were huge, so much bigger than I could have imagined, towering over our heads as we drove through the streets. Although the buildings were super elegant and pretty, my favorite thing in the city was the crosswalks. Whenever the walk signs came on, I could see people crossing the street at parallel lines on every block for as far as the eye could see. This was definitely something you could never see in Texas!

When we got to the building where Starscape was held, we didn't have to even double-check that we'd arrived at the right place because the building was almost completely swallowed up by crowds of students with their parents lining up to get registered.

My friends and I thanked the driver and got out of the taxi with our bags. There were separate check-in lines for each of our specialties. We split up, since we were all studying different things. Zeina got in the picture book line, I got in the graphic novel line, Carolina got in the game design line, and Emma got in the fashion design line with her mom.

At first my friends and I tried to keep talking to one another, but after repeating "What?" and "I can't hear you!" several times, we gave up. There were just too many people, and the lines were moving at different speeds. So we started texting one another instead.

Gigi, since your line is moving faster, feel free to tell me our room number when you have it, Zeina texted in our group chat. I want to go up to our room first and come down to get my welcome packet later when there aren't that many people.

Sounds good, I replied.

I hope our rooms are still somewhat close to each other even though we're not rooming together, sent Carolina with a sad-face emoji.

Yeah it'd suck if Carolina and I are a whole separate building from you guys, Emma added.

Since her line ended up moving the fastest, Emma got her packet first, and then shortly after, Carolina.

Okay I got building C, room 234, texted Emma.

Wait what?? replied Carolina. I got building C too, but room 568! That sucks, did they split us up? I'm gonna fight someone.

My heart pounded as I checked in and got my own welcome packet.

I got building A, room 1613, I sent to the group chat.

Oh dear, replied Zeina. I'll get my own packet now then and see what I get. Hang on, guys!

I went to go stand with Carolina while we waited for Zeina. Meanwhile, Emma and her mom talked to one of the volunteers. Emma looked angry, but luckily, she didn't actually fight anyone like she said she would.

When we all grouped up again, Emma told us, "They said that roommate assignment requests were only granted if we were in the same specialty. Otherwise, it's a free-for-all. Jeez, I wish they'd clarified that in the information packet."

"Yes, they were very unclear," Ms. Chang huffed.

"Well, they did say roommate preferences weren't guaranteed," Carolina said with a frown. "Darn, I thought they were just saying that in case there was an odd number of people or something.

I didn't think we would actually be living with complete strangers."

"Same here," replied Emma.

At that moment Zeina finally joined us. From her sad expression, I already knew what she was going to say.

"Gigi, we're not rooming together," she said. "I'm in building C, room three forty-five."

My heart sank, and my palms grew sweaty.

"Wait, why is everyone in building C while I'm in building A?" I asked.

My friends all looked at me, their sad expressions making me feel even worse.

My worst nightmare had come true. I was separated from all my friends!

Seven

We walked out of the building, away from all the lines and crowds. It was still kind of hard to hear them above the sound of traffic and passing people, but it was better than inside.

"Okay, so the good news is," Carolina said, "Zeina, Emma, and I are all in the same building, only a few floors away from each other. The bad news is . . ."

My friends all turned to look at me. I stared down

at my feet. Why did I have to be the one in a whole separate building from everyone else? It wouldn't have been so bad if the buildings were right next to each other, but according to the map, building A was on the entire other side of Washington Square from building C. I had to walk through a whole park to get to my friends!

"I'm sure we can all meet up elsewhere on campus," Zeina said, trying her best to be reassuring. "There's probably a cafeteria, right? Just like back at school. And we can also still go to the other cool places we wanted to go together while we're in the city, like the Met or Central Park!"

Emma patted me on my back. "Yeah, we'll still see you around, Gigi," she said.

"It really sucks that they didn't tell us you have to be in the same specialty as your roommate," Carolina said. "I've never shared my room before, much less with a stranger."

"Me neither," Emma said with a shrug. "But I feel

like it could be fun! I hope my roommate is cool."

"I just hope whoever rooms with me is respectful," Zeina said, matter-of-factly. "Like my sisters were and Gigi was in the times she slept over."

I looked sadly at Zeina. "I was hoping Starscape could be like our sleepovers."

Zeina matched my frown. "Me too! But it's okay. We can get through this!"

"Well, I guess we should get going," Carolina said, grabbing her suitcase. "Let's keep each other updated via the group chat!"

"Right." Zeina grabbed her things too. And so did Emma.

"Since Gigi has to walk across the park by herself, I'll walk her to her dorm and then head over to my sister's," Ms. Chang said. "I'm sorry to hear about the roommate situation, girls, but I hope you all still have a wonderful time. Remember, I'll be just a fifteen-minute subway ride away, so please feel free to text or call if you need anything."

"Will do," Zeina said. "Thank you, Ms. Chang!"

"Thanks, Mom!" Emma waved bye to her mom before she, Carolina, and Zeina set off in the opposite direction as me, to building C.

Before they were completely out of earshot, Emma looked back at me and waved. "Good luck, Gigi!" she exclaimed. "Don't die!"

"Emma!" Ms. Chang gasped in horror.

"Don't even joke like that!" Carolina yelled. "Your mom is going with her. She'll be fine."

"She's feeling bad about everything as it is!" Zeina hissed. "Let's not make things worse than they already are for her!"

With a sad smile, I waved bye to my friends and made the long trek across the park to building A with Ms. Chang. It probably wasn't that long, actual distance-wise, but because I had to walk away from my friends, it felt like I was going several miles away.

When I finally arrived at the building, I took a moment to gawk at how tall it was. Since my room number was 1613, I was probably on the sixteenth floor. Aside from when I stayed in my relatives' apartments in Korea, this was the first time I would be sleeping in such a tall building.

The one piece of good news was that all the rooms seemed to have windows. Even though it sucked that I was far away from all my friends, I was looking forward to the view of the city I'd have from my room.

"Best of luck, Gigi," Ms. Chang said after she walked me to the front entrance of the dorm. "I'm sure you'll be fine, but in case you're not, please don't hesitate to text or call."

"I definitely will," I said. "Thanks, Ms. Chang."

We waved bye and I entered the building. It took me a while to find where I was supposed to go, but soon enough, I was standing in front of room 1613.

Slowly, I opened the door. The room was smaller than my bedroom in Texas, but instead of just one bed, there were two squeezed in together. Aside from the beds, there was nothing much other than two desks, a microwave, and a mini-fridge. On the right side of the room, another Asian girl was already unpacking her stuff onto her desk. I assumed she was Korean, like me, because she was singing loudly in Korean while wearing a pair of big pink headphones. She must have had her volume way up since she didn't look up as I came in.

Not wanting to scare her, I slowly approached and waved my hand. But even when I was a few inches away from her, she still didn't notice me.

I tapped her on her shoulder. "Hi! My name is—"

She screamed, flinging her headphones off and leaping onto her bed.

I blushed, my finger still hovering in the air where her shoulder had been just moments ago.

"Hi," I said. "Sorry. I'm Gigi. I'm your roommate. It's nice to meet you!"

The girl made a face, like I was speaking too loud. "Gi . . . gi?" she asked, sounding out my name slowly.

"That's a name? My name is Sohee. Choi Sohee."

I bit my lip but tried my best to still sound friendly. "Yup! My full name is Ji-young. Ji-young Shin."

Sohee's mouth made an O shape. "Oh, you're Korean too? Hanguk mal hal jul ara?"

I hung out with my cousins back in Seoul enough times to know that she'd said, "Can you speak Korean?"

"A little," I said. "But I was born and raised in Texas, so not really."

"Texas!" Sohee's eyes went wide. "There are Korean people in Texas?"

"Quite a lot, actually!" I said. "I used to go to Korean school, and my family and I go to a Korean church. My parents also own a Korean grocery store."

"Grocery store?" Sohee asked with a frown. "Is that like a Super?"

I recognized that word from when I hung out with my cousins. Super, or *shu-puh,* like it was pronounced in Korean, was what some people called grocery stores.

"Yeah!"

Sohee made a face again, as if she thought I was weird. My heart fell. It'd been only five minutes and my roommate already thought I was strange. What had gone wrong?

"Um," I said, belatedly remembering that I hadn't asked Sohee about herself. "Where are you from?"

"Seoul" was all she said before she put her headphones back on.

Sohee and I didn't talk for the rest of the day as we unpacked and settled into our own sides of the room. Occasionally, as I got out my clothes and the rest of my things, I saw Sohee silently glancing over at me. I tried my best to keep my eyes glued to my own stuff, looking back at her only through my peripheral vision.

I texted my parents to let them know I'd safely arrived at my dorm, sent Paul an "I miss you" message on KakaoTalk, and then checked in with my friends in the group chat. But no one replied right away. It was four a.m. in Korea, so I didn't expect Paul to reply, and I guess everyone else was busy going about their day.

I'd never felt more alone in my life.

I touched the bracelet Paul had given me on the last day of school. Well, at least I knew I wasn't *completely* alone. Not really.

I was about to get out my sketchbook and draw when I got an incoming video call from Paul. After checking to see that Sohee still had her headphones on, I accepted the call.

"Hey," Paul said when I picked up. His surroundings were dark, and I could barely make out his face. But I could still see his big, warm smile. I felt instantly better.

"Hey!" I greeted him. "Isn't it four a.m. in Korea right now?"

"Yeah," Paul replied. "But I'm still so jet-lagged, I've been waking up in the middle of the night. How's NYC?"

"Good!" I answered automatically. But then I paused and said, "Well, the city is awesome. It still feels so surreal, in a good way. But . . . my friends and I all got split up, and I'm the only one from our friend group who is in this entire building. It's a whole park away from my friends. So that kind of sucks."

I wanted to go on and tell him about my awkward encounter with Sohee, but I didn't in case she was listening in.

"Aw man," Paul said, sounding genuinely disappointed for me. "That *does* really suck. I hope you can make new friends in your building, though. But if not, the camp is only a few weeks long, right?"

"It's a month long, but yeah," I said half-heartedly. Normally, I'd be eager to make new friends, but after Sohee's and my awkward encounter, I wasn't so sure I could make any anymore. My confidence was at an all-time low. "I never thought I'd say this, but I kind of miss Texas."

"Hang in there!" Paul said. "And feel free to call

me whenever you get lonely. Or text, whichever is easier. I can't guarantee I'll always answer right away, but I'll reply whenever I get the chance."

I smiled, feeling a lot better than I had before he called. "Thanks, Paul. What are you up to today? When everyone else is up, I mean."

"Honestly? I'm probably just going to eat a lot of good food. My entire family is jet-lagged, not just me, so the only thing we have planned today is to go to the night market later to eat some street food."

"That sounds like a lot of fun! Be sure to take lots of pics!"

"Will do," said Paul with a smile.

We were about to hang up when he lifted his left wrist so I could see his bracelet.

"Hey," he said. "By the way, I thought of you a lot today—well, I guess it's technically yesterday now since it's the middle of the night. But you know what I mean. I miss you lots."

"I miss you, too," I said. "The bracelet is helping,

though. It's making me feel less lonely. Thanks again for the good idea."

"You're welcome. Be sure to send me lots of pics of what you're up to, okay? I want to know all about Starscape and your classes and stuff."

I nodded. I wished I could squeeze Paul's hand. But since I couldn't right now, I squeezed my bracelet instead.

Eight

After the craziness of our first day in NYC, my friends and I managed to grab dinner together later that evening at a pizzeria near my dorm building.

It was my first time going to a New York–style pizza place. Back at home, my family rarely ate out, so when I did have pizza, it was usually at school or whenever my friends got pizza delivery from a popular chain like Papa Johns. The restaurant we were at right now was small, but it had a nice and cozy feel. The air inside also smelled so good, like breadsticks fresh out of the oven.

I stared, open-mouthed, as two men with burly arms quickly lifted pizzas in and out of the oven while a lady was taking orders in a quick New York accent. Everyone was moving *so* fast. It was a pace I wasn't used to from living in Texas all my life.

I got two slices of pepperoni pizza. They were so fresh that the cheese and tomato sauce were still bubbling from being in the oven. Zeina got a vegetarian pizza, while Emma got cheese, and Carolina got meatball.

There were only a handful of tables and chairs in front of the counter, and they were all full except one table. My friends and I sat down at the last remaining table and started eating our pizzas.

For a brief moment it felt like we were back in our school cafeteria lunch table in Texas. I let out a slow breath, relaxing for the first time the entire day since my friends and I got on the plane to NYC this morning.

"So, how's everyone's roommate?" asked Carolina in between bites.

"Mine is really shy," said Zeina. "Even shyer than me. I think she also likes books, though. I'm trying to figure out if we have any favorites in common. So far, the only ones we both like are the Percy Jackson books."

"That's nice!" said Carolina. "I'm not sure if I have a roommate. She hasn't shown up yet. I kind of hope she doesn't."

"Lucky!" Emma said. "My roommate is so loud and obnoxious. She just goes on and on about all the cute artsy boys she's going to kiss and how she wants to be the next Anna Wintour. She won't stop talking!"

We all stared at Emma. She stared back at us before her mouth formed a small O. We all burst out laughing.

Emma put a hand over her mouth, but I could tell

she was still grinning. "I'm not that bad, am I? I've at least never compared myself to Anna Wintour."

"No, you haven't," Carolina admitted. "But you have to admit some of that does sound familiar."

Emma laughed. "Okay, fair. But, gosh, if I'm ever that annoying, feel free to slap me!"

Carolina raised her eyebrows. "Okay, but remember, you asked for it!"

Still smiling, Zeina turned to me and asked, "How about you, Gigi? How's your roommate?"

"Well, she's from Seoul, which is where my cousins live," I replied. "I'm not sure if she speaks much English, and we didn't exactly get off on the right foot. I think she already thinks I'm weird. She keeps giving me these strange looks."

"Did you tell her you're Korean too?" Carolina asked.

"Yeah! The thing is, I think she judged me a lot less when she didn't know I was *Korean* American. But now that she knows, it's like I opened a can of worms."

"That's so weird!" Emma said. "But I can relate. That's kind of how my cousins treat me whenever they visit from Taiwan. I think some people from Asia just really find us Asian Americans weird, like we're impostors or something."

"Whew," I said. "So it isn't just me. My cousins don't treat me that way, but maybe it's because they're more used to me and Tommy being the way we are."

"Yeah, maybe this is her first time meeting a Korean American! She probably just needs time to get used to you."

"You know, I didn't even ask her if this is her first time in the US. I should probably ask her that, huh?"

"Yeah!" Zeina said. "That can be a good conversation opener."

She gave me an encouraging smile.

I nodded. Maybe I should try talking to Sohee again after all.

"Did you guys take a look at your schedules yet?" Carolina asked, changing the subject. "I have my very first class tomorrow with R. J. Simmons. He's, like, one of my favorite game designers of all time!"

"That's awesome!" Zeina said. "My first class is with an author-illustrator named Jackie Smith. She makes these adorable picture books about dogs, so that's going to be really cute."

"Oh my gosh, that sounds amazing," Emma replied. "I don't know the person who's teaching my class tomorrow, but apparently she worked for a bunch of top fashion brands, so that's exciting."

While listening to my friends talk about their schedules, I had a terrifying realization. I'd been so sad over the whole roommate thing that I forgot to check my schedule!

I quickly opened the welcome folder I'd stashed in my bag.

Tomorrow at ten a.m. I had class with Christiana Moon, my favorite graphic novelist! My dreams were coming true!

"My first class is with Christiana Moon!" I exclaimed, jumping up from my seat.

A few people around us turned to give us concerned looks, so I said, "Sorry!"

I sat back down, my heart pounding. Christiana Moon was the entire reason I wanted to go to Starscape in the first place. A famous comic book artist, she created *Waterfall,* my favorite graphic novel of all time. Since I usually just used the library, I only owned a handful of books, but my copy of *Waterfall #1* was tattered and worn.

The icing on the cake was she was also friends with my aunt Yeji! Or, at least, I think they're friends. I saw an Instagram post once where Christiana and Yeji were hanging out together.

My friends and I went on to talk about all the classes we were excited about this month. By the time we all said goodbye and I walked down the street to my dorm building, I had a big smile on my face. This past year, my friends and I worked so hard, tutoring almost every day after school to get to where we are now. I was so proud of us. We really did it!

LYLA LEE

So what if my roommate situation was less than ideal? I didn't come to New York to make new friends; I came here to learn how to become a better artist from experts like Christiana Moon! Sure, I was separated from my friends, but we could still hang out together like we did today.

I had to keep in mind why I came here in the first place. And even though my friends weren't rooming with me, I had to remember we were all in this experience together.

Nine

I woke up to a bunch of pictures Paul had sent me of the different foods he'd tried at the night market in Seoul. He'd tried everything from tornado potatoes to the more traditional snacks like steamed red bean buns. My mouth watered. I wished I was in Seoul too.

I sent back a bunch of heart-eyed emojis and headed to my first class at Starscape.

When I walked into the classroom and saw

LYLA LEE

Christiana Moon perched elegantly on a stool at the front, my jaw almost dropped to the floor. After months—no, *years*—of following her on Instagram and seeing news articles about her all the time online, I had to pinch myself to even come to terms with the fact that she was really physically right there. She was in the same room as me, breathing the same air I was!

Christiana was dressed in an elegant red suit with a white blouse underneath. She looked so cool, like she'd just walked out of a New York fashion show. From where I was standing, I could see that she was on her phone, flipping through photos to post on Instagram. I didn't want to bother her, so I walked quietly around her stool to find a seat at one of the other tables in the room. Each table had two seats, and all the chairs were already occupied except one.

In the very back, Sohee was sitting by herself. Everyone else must have been sitting with their roommates.

I sat down next to her.

"Hi," I said.

Sohee gave me a small grin and scooted her stuff over a little to make room. But she didn't say hi back.

"Okay, everyone," said Christiana. I'd heard her voice many times before on my phone since she frequently did voice-overs for her reels. In real life, she sounded a bit different; her voice was higher than what I was used to. But maybe we all sounded a bit different online and offline? She still looked as cool as she did in the photos, though.

"Hi, my name is Christiana Moon, and I have the great pleasure of teaching your first session at Starscape. This class is going to be about graphic novels, but you all probably already know that. Or, at least, I hope you do."

She stopped to give us all a dazzling grin and some people—including me—laughed at her joke.

"Raise your hands if you've ever drawn your own comics before," she continued.

Almost everyone in the room, including me and Sohee, raised their hands.

"Excellent. And how many of you have made your own graphic novels? Complete works with a beginning, middle, and end?"

I didn't expect anyone to raise their hands, but several of the other kids, including Sohee, did. *Already?* I looked around the room, trying to wrap my head around how they could have possibly done so much when they were still around the same age as me.

"Amazing. I expected nothing less from such a talented group. In that case, I'm going to skip a lot of the introductory material and go into the more challenging concepts. The last thing I want to do is bore you all."

I gulped. I wanted to stand up and yell, *Wait! I need the boring beginner stuff!* But I was too embarrassed to say anything. Everyone else, including Sohee, just nodded, so I nodded, too.

The only comic-book-making experience I had was drawing short panels of Meteor Girl and her friends. I'd never made an actual comic book before and had no idea how to even start. I thought this class was where I'd learn that exact thing!

"All right, then, excellent," Christiana continued. "This class is designed to help you create your own graphic novels, so I will be mostly hands-off except when giving feedback on assignments. And in order to give you all the freedom needed to stretch your creative muscles as artists, I won't be making rounds unless absolutely necessary. I trust all of you to be on task, since this isn't just your normal art class in school where the teacher has to hold your hand and make sure you are working every day. We're all motivated to become better artists here, correct?"

Everyone said, "Yes!" or eagerly nodded.

I couldn't bring myself to answer with everyone else. I was too worried about what Christiana had just said. In the description on the Starscape website, it'd sounded like her class would be an actual class, not just a workshop where we'd be working by ourselves all day. My art teacher back at school, Ms. Williams, always guided us through everything and made sure no one was lost or confused. I suddenly felt really homesick.

"Of course, I don't expect you to finish an entire book in a month," Christiana said with a laugh. "You will all have the opportunity to present whatever you finish and feel comfortable sharing at the Starscape Student Showcase at the end of this program. Presentations are not mandatory, but the showcase is largely recognized and attended by faculty members of prominent art schools, so I highly recommend you present. You can either choose to present by yourselves or with a group of other students at Starscape."

We all looked at one another. Some people nodded and pointed at each other, like they already knew who they wanted to group up with for the showcase. I looked at Sohee, but she avoided my gaze. Well, I guess I wasn't presenting with her.

I made a mental note to ask my friends about the showcase later.

"You are, of course, always welcome to come up to the front to ask me questions at any time," Christiana went on. "That's what I'm here for. There will also be check-ins every Friday to make sure you're on the right track. For this week's, I will check your story outlines and your first few pages. Feel free to share more than that if you end up working ahead. Does anyone have any questions?"

Again no one else said anything, so I stayed quiet too, even though I had a million confused thoughts bouncing around in my head.

And that was that. Christiana said, "Excellent. Please get started," and went back to staring at her phone.

Everyone else seemed to know exactly what to do. They all started working right away, grabbing paper and other supplies from the back of the room before going back to their seats.

Sohee immediately pulled up a picture on her phone and started sketching it in her sketchbook. I snuck a glance at it and gasped. For her first panel, she was drawing a beautiful Korean royal palace. Even though she'd only drawn a few lines, it already looked so good, like something straight out of a K-drama!

After a few minutes of just sitting there, I finally mustered up the courage to talk to Christiana. I stood up from my seat and walked the entire length of the classroom to her, my feet heavy and my heart thumping loudly in my chest. This was going to be my first time talking to a celebrity, so I had no idea how I was supposed to even start our conversation.

Finally, after going through a bunch of possibilities while I approached her stool, I decided that a simple greeting was probably best.

"H-hi," I said when I was close enough for her to

hear me. My voice trembled, and I let out a quick breath to steady myself before going on. "My name is Gigi Shin. I think you know my aunt? Her name is Yeji Park."

Christiana's eyes widened a little with recognition. "Oh yes, I know Yeji. I had no idea her niece was going to be in my class. It's nice to meet you, Gigi. I expect great things from you."

Oh no. My palms grew sweaty.

"Um, about that," I said. "So I've actually never drawn a full-length graphic novel by myself before, so I don't even know how to begin."

Christiana's eyes narrowed a little, making my heart skip a beat. "Is that so?" she said. "I thought all the students who got admitted to this program were required to have experience."

I gulped. "I do have experience. I've made short comic book panels before but never a whole book with one cohesive story."

"I see. Well, in that case, Gigi, I suggest writing

the story first, in script format. If you haven't done so already."

"Oh, okay," I said. "And how do I do that?"

Christiana frowned again. "There are plenty of guides on how to do that online. I can't hold your hand through everything, you know. I'm afraid I can't give you special treatment just because I know your aunt."

"Oh, no, that's not what I . . ." I trailed off as my eyes welled up with tears. I felt like a kicked puppy. I barely even knew Yeji-imo and had only mentioned my aunt to say hi. But somehow I'd already given Christiana a completely wrong first impression of myself! I wished I could go back in time and redo this entire conversation.

"Sorry," I said. "Thanks for the help."

Turning quickly away before I started bawling in front of the entire class, I rushed back to our table, where Sohee had set aside her drawing to type some things on her tablet. Everything she wrote was in Korean, and although I knew some basic words, I couldn't understand anything on her screen. She was using words I'd never learned in Korean school.

Even though I couldn't understand what she was writing, it was clear from the formatting of her document that she was working on a script, just like Christiana had told me to do. I thought of asking Sohee for help, but I was too afraid to talk to her. After *our* rocky first meeting, who knew how she'd react when I asked for help?

I looked around the room and noticed that a lot of the other kids had tablets with them. Everyone around me was either busily writing or drawing. No one else was just sitting there, looking lost and confused, like I was. Was I the only one who hadn't come prepared with a whole story already?

This was a worst-nightmare scenario. Trying not to panic, I got out my sketchbook.

It's okay, I told myself. *It's not like I have to start completely from scratch. I have Meteor Girl and her friends. I just need to figure out a story for them.*

I didn't have a tablet, so I used my phone to look up a bunch of tutorials on script writing, just like Christiana had suggested. It was hard to understand anything at first, but by the end of class, I felt like I got the hang of it.

I got out a notebook I sometimes used to jot down ideas and flipped to a blank page. Just when I was about to write some random ideas down, Christiana said, "Okay, class, that's it for today. I'll see you at the same time tomorrow!"

I'd only managed to just stare down at my paper! Meanwhile, some people like Sohee had written multiple pages of their scripts or even started drawing already.

I only had until Friday to come up with an idea, write out a story, and draw the first few pages. I was doomed!

Ten

When I asked my friends about the showcase, they already had a lot of ideas about what they wanted to do.

"I have some ideas on some clothes I can make," Emma said when we met back up at the pizza place for lunch. "How about you guys?"

Carolina nodded. "Same here. Well, the having ideas part, not the clothes part. I'll probably make a really short video game that people can play as they're passing through."

"That's cool," said Zeina. "I started a new book recently, so I'll probably display an excerpt from that."

When it was my turn to share, I took a bite out of my deluxe pizza and chewed slowly, so I had more time to think. The four of us all had different pizzas from the ones we had last time. Emma got the buffalo chicken, Carolina got the pepperoni, and Zeina got the cheese. At this rate, we'd be able to try all the different pizzas available at this restaurant before we returned to Texas.

"All your ideas sound really great," I said when I was done chewing. "I'm probably going to share something out of the comic book I'm making for Christiana's class. But I have no idea how to even begin."

"You still have a lot of time," Zeina assured me. "Today's only the first day!"

I nodded, trying to think positively. But just thinking about Christiana's class this morning made me almost lose my appetite. Everything had gone so terribly wrong!

Besides Christiana's class, I was also in a general drawing class on Tuesdays and a creative writing class with Zeina and Carolina on Wednesdays. It was such a big relief to know that I had at least *some* overlap with my friends.

The writing class was taught by Mr. Hernandez, a children's book author who lived in Brooklyn. I thought I wouldn't like his class since it was all about words and not pictures or drawing, but it was my favorite class at Starscape so far.

"Always remember, friends," he said at the end of our first session. "We can find inspiration in the everyday. The best writers are the ones who reflect reality, whether in recognizable forms or not."

On our way out of the classroom, I was still

thinking about what he'd said when Carolina waved her hand in front of my face. "Hello?" she said. "Did you hear what I said?"

"Huh?"

"Guess not. Well, anyway, Zeina, Emma, me, and a whole bunch of other people in building C are going out to get ice cream tonight. The shop is literally across the street from the pizza place we went to. You wanna come?"

I wanted to nod so badly that my neck ached slightly. But I couldn't. I'd tried my best on Monday and Tuesday, but I still hadn't even come up with the story for the graphic novel for Christiana's class. Now I had just two days to not only come up with the idea but also draw the first few pages.

"Or you could come with us to get bagels tomorrow morning!" Zeina added. "Emma said she and her mom know a really good place nearby."

My friends waited for my response. I took a deep breath. But instead of saying yes like I desperately wanted to, I said, "I can't make it to either place. I really want to, but I have to work on my graphic novel for Christiana Moon's class. I haven't even figured out what the story is going to be about yet."

I'd complained about the project enough times in the group chat that my friends sadly nodded in understanding.

"It's okay," Carolina said. "We can hang out some other time, then! Good luck with the assignment!"

I holed myself up in my dorm room for the rest of the day, thinking about what Mr. Hernandez had said about "reflecting reality." The closest thing I'd done to that was when I drew my panels about Meteor Girl and her friends, my comic book superhero characters that were based on me and *my* friends. But what could I write for the full story?

I wished I could ask someone for help, but after our terrible conversation on the first day, I didn't want to make Christiana mad again. And things between

Sohee and me were awkward as usual, while my aunt Yeji hadn't ever replied to the text I sent her when I first arrived in NYC. At this rate, I wasn't sure if we were even going to hang out anymore.

I fell asleep trying to brainstorm ideas and woke up in the middle of the night, still at my desk. When I slowly crawled into bed, inspiration finally struck. I could write about how Meteor Girl was stuck in New York City all by herself, separated by an invisible force field that kept her from all her friends! It was the biggest challenge she faced yet, and the only way she could escape was to figure out a way to use her powers to the fullest.

Once I got that initial idea down, I was able to work through everything else. By ten a.m. on Friday, I showed up to Christiana's class with not only the script outline but also the first few pages I'd sketched out. It wasn't much, but it was something. And definitely way more than I thought I could do on Monday.

Christiana walked around the room to look at all our pages. When she came to our table, she oohed and aahed at Sohee's work.

"This is phenomenal," she said. "You're such a talented artist, and I'm captivated by the story already."

Sohee gave Christiana a small smile. "Thank you," she said quietly.

When Christiana came to me, she frowned. "Superheroes?"

I nodded. "Yes, this is Meteor Girl. It's one of my original characters."

She didn't even look past the first page before she said, "Gigi, can you please come speak with me at my desk? I want to talk to you about something."

Sohee's eyes widened. The people around us gasped and whispered.

I bit my lip. "Sure."

When I arrived at her desk, Christiana asked, "Gigi, why did you come to Starscape?"

I let out a quick breath. My reasons for wanting

to come to Starscape had been so firm in my head while I was applying. I wanted to learn from the very best like Christiana herself. I wanted to go to a summer art camp with my friends. I wanted all of us to grow as artists.

Although the last reason was probably still possible, the rest had become a bit murky.

"Well, I want to grow as an artist and become a professional graphic novelist as an adult," I said at last.

"And how are you supposed to grow if you just keep drawing the same characters over and over again?" she asked. "I looked into your application during the week and saw that you drew these characters then as well. Plus, superheroes are so . . . overdone. Even Marvel movies are starting to feel antiquated nowadays. Can't you just work on your superhero comics at home by yourself?"

"Um—"

But before I could explain that I *was* still challenging myself to grow as she suggested, since this was my first time making a full-on graphic novel with an entire story and everything, Christiana went on. "And I'm sorry to say this, but your story is rather juvenile, and your art style could also use some work. It's great for a seventh grader, but you're in the big leagues now. I suggest you practice your line art drawing skills a bit more. Some of the lines are very sloppy."

I went numb from head to toe.

"Um, okay," I said quietly. "Thank you."

"I want you to take the weekend to really think about what kind of story you want to tell," Christiana continued. "Starting over might be challenging, but trust me when I say it'll be worth it."

I bit my lip. I'd worked so hard this past week to even come up with this idea in the first place. And now I had to start over?

I tightened my hands into fists. Even though I did appreciate Christiana's honest feedback, I couldn't help but feel a little annoyed. I wished she'd actually

LYLA LEE

taught us things during classes so I had a better idea of what we were supposed to do in the first place.

But since I didn't want to make a big fuss, I just replied, "Okay, understood."

I managed to hold everything in until I was back in my dorm room. And then, finally, when I was in my bed, I let everything go. I was sobbing into my pillow when I heard a knock on the frame of my bed.

"Hey," Sohee said. "Are you okay?"

I looked up and was surprised to see her standing next to me with a worried look on her face. This was the only time she'd started a conversation with me in this whole first week of classes. Although I was grateful that she'd come to check in on me, I almost wish she hadn't. My nose was full of snot, and my cheeks were streaked with tears. I was a mess!

Luckily, Sohee didn't say anything as she handed me a box of tissues. I took one and blew my nose before replying, "Not really. Christiana hated the work I did."

"She's a tough critic. Don't feel too bad!"

"But what if it's just me being bad? She seemed to really love your work."

Sohee looked away shyly. "I think she was just really impressed by my line art skills."

I remembered what Christiana said about my lines being "sloppy." Suddenly, I wanted to see how Sohee's and mine compared.

"If it's okay with you, can I see what you've done so far?"

"Um, sure." She showed me her sketches. I was absolutely floored by the art. Sohee's style reminded me of the Korean webtoons I read. Her drawings were cartoony, but they were still precise, with the lines exact and clear, like a professional's. I could see why Christiana had been praising her so much in class.

"This is amazing!" I exclaimed. "You're so talented!"

"Thanks," Sohee said, looking slightly uncomfortable like she had when Christiana praised her in class. She coughed and asked, "Do you know why Christiana hated your work?"

"Well, apparently she doesn't even like my idea. She also said I need more practice drawing in general. According to her, I should start completely over."

"Wow, that sucks."

Sohee paused in thought before continuing. "You know, what I like to do back in Seoul is go to museums. They always give me a lot of inspiration for new art when I need it. And sometimes I just sit in front of the artworks and draw all day. It helps me a lot. Maybe it can help you, too?"

Suddenly I remembered one of the drawings I'd submitted to Starscape. It was of Meteor Girl standing at the steps of the Met. Back then I'd had no idea I would even have the chance to go to the famous museum in person. But now . . .

I pulled up Google Maps and searched for directions to the Met from our dorm. Back in Texas, our local big museum was too far from our neighborhood for us to go without our parents, but the Met was only a fifteen-minute subway ride and twelve-minute walk away!

Sohee had gone back to being on her bed, where she was scrolling through her phone with her headphones on. Come to think of it, whenever I was in my room, Sohee was too. And she was probably also still here when I left to go hang out with my friends. I wasn't sure if she knew anyone here besides me at all.

So, in spite of the awkward first conversation we had, I thought of how nice she'd been to me just now and waved at her.

"Hey," I said when she took off her headphones. "I'm thinking of going to the Met with my friends. Do you wanna come hang out with us? They're all in Starscape too, just in different specialties."

Sohee immediately put her phone down and sat up, her eyes wide with surprise.

"Really?" she asked.

"Yeah! You're welcome to join if you want."

"Oh . . . sure!" she said, looking genuinely happy. "I do. Let's go."

I smiled. I'd thought Sohee didn't want to be friends with me because she thought I was weird, but maybe she was just shy and needed some time to get used to me, like Emma had said. Hopefully we could put our awkward first conversation behind us and get closer to becoming friends.

Does anyone want to go to the Met with me? I texted the group chat with my friends.

Zeina replied right away. **YES! I was hoping to go soon.**

Emma was second to reply. **Yuh yuh! They have a cool fashion exhibit going on right now that I wanted to check out. It'll also probably give us good ideas for the showcase. I'll ask my mom if she's free to go with us, since the subway might not be safe.**

Carolina replied a few minutes later. **Down.**

Also is it okay if I bring Sohee, my roommate? I added to the group chat.

Yeah, the more the merrier! Zeina replied.

Thanks to Sohee and my friends, I suddenly had a faint glimmer of hope that I could overcome Christiana's challenging class. And all things considered, why couldn't I? I worked hard and was able to get to Starscape in the first place, even when my parents couldn't afford to send me here. What's to say I wouldn't be able to get myself out of this predicament too?

Luckily, Emma told us that her mom could take us on Saturday. It was only my first weekend in NYC, and it was already shaping up to be a great one!

Eleven

The Met was almost sparkling white in the bright sunlight and bigger than I could have ever imagined from the pictures I'd seen online. It looked more like a majestic castle than the museum, and Zeina, Sohee, Carolina, and I gasped as we took lots of pictures of the building from all sorts of different angles.

"Isn't the Met absolutely gorgeous?" Ms. Chang

smiled as she and Emma watched us take pictures. "I recommend you girls look up at the columns to fully take in all the intricate details."

"Yeah, they're really cool," Emma said. "I think I stayed outside just staring at the building for fifteen minutes when my mom and I first came here."

I had to pinch myself repeatedly to make sure I wasn't dreaming. I couldn't quite believe that we were actually *right here*, on the same steps that celebrities walked up every year for the Met Gala. The same steps that I'd seen on my aunt Yeji's Instagram.

Since we'd all rushed to get on the subway, I hadn't gotten a chance to properly introduce Sohee to my friends. So once we finished taking in the awesomeness of the Met, I said, "Oh, yeah, Sohee, these are my friends from back in Texas. This is Ms. Chang, Emma's mom. She came with us on this trip. Everyone, this is Sohee, my roommate."

"Nice to meet you, Sohee!" said Zeina. "Glad you could join us."

Sohee blushed a little and said, "It's nice to meet you all too!"

We were about to go in when Emma yelled, "Wait! We have to take a big group picture on the steps! To commemorate our trip to NYC together."

Sohee backed away. "Oh, I can take the picture for you guys if you want."

"Nonsense, dear," Ms. Chang said. "I can take the picture for you girls. Gather around and strike a pose!"

We did what she said. I grinned big and wide. I'd dreamed of this exact moment.

"Cute!" Ms. Chang said after she took the picture.

As impressive as the Met had been on the outside, the inside of the museum was somehow even more mind-boggling. The ceilings were super high, and there was a massive staircase that ran through the center of the museum's front area.

Ms. Chang bought us our tickets and we started wandering around. It was so surreal to see art in person that I'd only seen as posters in Ms. Williams's class, like Degas's ballerinas and *Washington Crossing the Delaware*. Many of the art pieces were either so much bigger or smaller than they had looked in prints and books.

Also unbelievable was the huge courtyard with ancient Greek sculptures from several thousands of years ago. My friends and I took as many pictures together as we could, and Emma made everyone laugh by posing dramatically with the sculptures.

I'd seen a lot of the artwork in the Met on TV, in classes, and on Google Images plenty of times before, but none of that compared to the experience of having everything right in front of me. All the art was so *real* and powerful. Thinking about all the different artists from all over the world who had created the art throughout thousands of years was overwhelming in a good way.

When it was almost time for us to go back to Starscape, we decided to split into groups so everyone could see what they wanted to see.

Carolina, Sohee, and Zeina went to the medieval European and Asian art sections while Emma, Ms. Chang, and I went to the modern art and fashion special exhibits.

"Let's meet back up at the main hall in thirty minutes, girls," Ms. Chang said. "Hope everyone enjoys the rest of their time in the museum!"

I didn't think I'd be too impressed by the modern art section, but the moment I entered the room, I was taken aback by all the different creative pieces. My favorite was Jackson Pollock's painting. Although at first glance, it just seemed like a bunch of paint splatters, the more I stared at it, the more I noticed the great care he must have taken to create the artwork.

Sohee had been right. By the time we left the museum, I was bursting with ideas for my assignment.

Later that night, I lay in my bed. Whenever I closed my eyes, I saw the different works of art I'd seen at the Met.

I thought about how Jackson Pollock, Vincent van Gogh, and other artists had their own unique styles and painted whatever they wanted, even when people said what they were doing wasn't art. Even though I still had a long way to go and was nowhere near those great artists, I still felt really inspired. It made me think about my own art and about how I'd been drawing superhero comics for as long as I could remember. Even if they were "overdone" like Christiana had said, none of the other books were about Meteor Girl and her friends. And none of them were by me or about the story I wanted to tell. Didn't that mean they were still worth pursuing?

Plus, Christiana had been so dismissive. Not only was she on her phone for most of class, but she hadn't given me anything but bad feedback. It made me wonder if she really cared about me or the rest of the students in our class.

After glancing across the room to make sure Sohee wasn't sleeping yet—she was thankfully just listening to music with her headphones on while drawing—I video called Paul and told him about my dilemma.

"On the one hand, I can listen to Christiana and start working on something else," I summarized for him at the end. "Or on the other, I can trust my instincts and go with what I had before."

"Hm, that sounds like a tough decision, Gigi," said Paul. "I'm no expert on art or anything like that, but I personally think you should just do whatever you want. It's your story, and it's your graphic novel! Not Christiana's."

"That's true. I guess I feel like I should go with what she told me to do since she's my teacher and this super-famous artist, you know? What if she's right about my idea being overdone?"

Paul shrugged. "She may be super famous, but she's just one person. She's also not you! And you'll probably never see her again after this month. If you think the story is bad, you can always fix it. But you should do whatever you want. It's not like you get grades there like we do in school, anyway."

We went on to talk about other things, like what Paul had been up to in Korea.

"There are so many cool museums and cute cafés here. And some things are so much more high tech. It's like living in the future!" he said. "My uncle has this cool closet that looks like a fridge. It steams and cleans his clothes so they're ready for work the next day."

"Wow, that's really cool! I can't even imagine having that in my house in Texas."

I'd never seriously thought about visiting Korea for anything besides family stuff before, but now I wanted to try going for fun, too. Paul seemed to be having the best time!

When we finished talking, I was about to hang up when Paul said, "Hey, Gigi?"

"Yeah?"

"About Starscape and Christiana's class . . . you'll figure it out, okay? I believe in you. You're a super-talented artist. Don't let her get you down."

I smiled. "I won't," I said. "Thanks, Paul."

Encouraged by our conversation, I thought of another story idea, thinking about what Mr. Hernandez had said during his class about "reflecting reality." I jotted down my idea right before I went to sleep. This time my graphic novel was about a girl named Melanie. Melanie was Meteor Girl after she lost her powers and found herself stranded in NYC. And she had to somehow get her powers back, something she could only do with the help of her friends.

When I was done, I began drawing the pages, starting off the story where my friends and I were this morning, at the steps of the Met. Melanie finds herself there, without her powers or her memories. I didn't know how the story was going to end yet, but I felt like I had a good start.

The next morning I showed it to Sohee, who gasped. "This is so good!'" she said after she read my outline and looked at my beginning sketches.

"Thanks!" I said.

I was about to go to sleep that night when I got a text. It was from Aunt Yeji!

Hey, Gigi! The text said. Are you free next Saturday for brunch? I'd love to meet you then!

My heart almost launched itself out of my mouth with excitement.

OF COURSE! I replied. I'll see you then.

Great 😊 Hope you're having a good time at Starscape!

When I went to bed, I was happier than I'd been since arriving at camp. Things were finally starting to look up!

Twelve

By Wednesday, I was already halfway done with my script. It wasn't going to be a full-length graphic novel or anything, but the entire story was probably going to be around thirty pages, which was the longest story I'd ever written. In Mr. Hernandez's class, we had some time to do independent work, so my friends and I shared what we were doing for our other classes. Zeina was working on a super-cute picture book about a cat and a dog that were frenemies but were learning to become actual friends, while Carolina was writing the story for a cool puzzle game about fighting robots in space. Both their projects looked amazing and so very *them* that it made my heart all fuzzy inside.

When I shared what I had so far, Zeina exclaimed, "Wow. This is unlike anything else I've seen you work on before, Gigi!"

"Yeah, it's like on a whole other level," added Carolina.

At that moment Mr. Hernandez overheard what my friends said and came over to our table with a big smile on his face.

"Do you mind if I take a look at what you're working on, Gigi?" he asked.

"Um, sure!" I handed my laptop over to the teacher, and he gently took it out of my hands. I bit my lip, feeling super self-conscious. After what had happened the last time I shared my work with a teacher, I was nervous about sharing it with anyone.

Mr. Hernandez slowly scrolled through the document. As he did, I watched his face carefully for his reactions, but his expression was completely unreadable. I couldn't tell if he liked what he read or not until he set the laptop down. His poker face finally disappeared, and a big smile slowly spread across his face. "Gigi, this is phenomenal. Definitely keep working on this story. I can see you've put so much of your heart and soul into this project."

I beamed. "What you said last class about reflecting reality helped a ton. It inspired me to write this story!"

"Amazing," he said. "I'm so glad to hear I could help. That's what I'm here for, after all. You girls are all presenting at the showcase at the end of this month, right? You really should consider it if you haven't already since it'll be an excellent opportunity."

My friends and I all nodded.

"We are," Carolina said.

"Excellent," Mr. Hernandez said. "I'm looking forward to seeing all of your amazing work there."

After Mr. Hernandez's class, I felt so much better

about my work that I got so much done later that night. By Friday I had the whole script done, along with the pencil sketches for the first ten pages. Before I went to Christiana's class, I showed my parents what I'd done over video chat. I almost *never* showed my parents my art, but thanks to the good feedback I received from Mr. Hernandez and my friends, I felt confident enough to give them a little peek.

"You improved so much in such a short time!" exclaimed Mom. "I'm glad the camp has been good for you."

"Yes, it seems like the camp has been worthwhile so far," agreed Dad.

This was one of the first times ever that my parents complimented my art. I beamed.

"Thanks!" I said.

"Take pictures of what you've drawn so far and send them to me," Mom said. "So I can show them to Yeji-imo."

Just the thought of my aunt Yeji seeing my work made me sweat, but I did what Mom said anyway.

Before I got a reply from Mom or Aunt Yeji, I had to go to Christiana's class again.

When it was my turn, Christiana frowned as she started flipping through my pages. Unlike with Mr. Hernandez, it was clear from the very beginning exactly what she thought of my work.

"Gigi, I thought we had an agreement that superheroes were overrated," she said.

I took a deep breath and told her the response I'd practiced by myself in the mirror, "That was your opinion, not mine. This is the story I feel the most strongly about."

"I see." Without even looking at the rest of the story, Christiana handed my pages back to me. "Then I'm afraid you may not be the right fit for my class. Here we value students who challenge themselves and are not afraid to try new things. Not do the same thing repeatedly."

"But she did try a new thing!" Sohee said before I could respond. "You told her she needs to have a better story, and that's exactly what she did. And her art improved as much as it could in a week's time. I've seen her working so hard on this every day."

I looked to Sohee, my eyes almost welling up with tears because of how grateful I felt.

"Hm, maybe so," Christiana said. "I suppose I can't really tell you what you can or can't draw. But it's still important to branch out and try new things, especially as a young artist."

"This is my first graphic novel," I replied. "Ever. I *am* challenging myself and trying new things."

Christiana shrugged. "In any case, your line art *has* become better. In such a short amount of time, too. Keep up with the good work, then."

She walked away. Sohee looked angry for me, but I said, "It's okay. At the end of the day, this is just Christiana's opinion. Thanks so much for defending me, though."

"You should keep working on this book," Sohee said. "And definitely present it during the showcase. See what the other experts who aren't Christiana have to say. Even after Starscape, if you don't finish it during the program, you should finish it and publish it one day! Don't let Christiana discourage you."

I smiled, grateful that I had a new friend like Sohee.

"Don't worry," I said. "I won't."

"Maybe we can dedicate some time to practice drawing together? We pretty much already sit quietly at our desks drawing every day in our room, so why not?"

"Like roommate-bonding drawing sessions? I love that idea!"

When we got back to our dorm, Sohee and I worked together for the rest of the day, listening to K-pop as we bonded over our favorite K-dramas and webtoons. It turned out that Sohee had read and watched some of the same things I had, just without

English subtitles like I did. Christiana's class may have been a bust so far, but I was so glad and grateful that I now had Sohee as a friend.

Later that night, I'd just gotten into my bed when I got a text.

Wow, Gigi! It was from Aunt Yeji. **Your mom sent me pictures of your work and I have to say, I'm really impressed! Listen, one of my friends is a professor at Parsons. I know it's still too early for you to seriously look into colleges but I think it'd be good for you to meet her. Do you mind if I invite her to our brunch tomorrow?**

My jaw dropped. Parsons wasn't my number one dream school like Tisch was, but it was still really cool.

Sure! I replied. **Thanks so much, Yeji-imo!**

I was so excited for tomorrow that I could hardly sleep.

Thirteen

The next morning, I was getting ready to go to brunch with Aunt Yeji when I got a text.

Hi, Gigi. So sorry but Diana—my friend—said she can't do today. Does the 25th work for you by any chance? She's free then so maybe we can eat dinner that PM.

The twenty-fifth was the night of the Starscape Showcase. My friends and I had all agreed to go together to support each other and present our work. It wasn't ideal, but maybe I could have dinner with them and then rush back to campus for the event.

Sure! I replied. I have an event back at camp at 7 so maybe we can do sometime before that?

Sounds good. I'll ask Diana and let you know what she says.

Suddenly I was totally free for the rest of the day. On the other side of the room, Sohee was at her desk, doing pretty much the same thing we did last night.

As I watched her work, I got a sudden idea. Besides the Met, there was one other place I really wanted to go with my friends. Since the Met visit had been so fun, I wanted to plan another outing with all five of us.

After asking Sohee if she was free—she was—I sent a text to my friends from home.

Hey, are you guys doing anything in the afternoon today? I wrote in our group chat. **Do you wanna go to Central Park with Sohee and me?**

Carolina was the first to reply. **I have something going on** with my video game class friends, but you guys go ahead without me!

My heart fell. But then Zeina replied, I'm down! Wanna meet in front of the subway station and ride the subway to the park together?

Emma was the last to chime in, a few minutes later.

I'm down too! My mom said she'll meet us at the station.

When we arrived at Central Park, I was surprised by everything around us. Tall skyscrapers peeked out past the horizon, something we could never see in our hometown. Actual horses trotted past us, pulling carriages. People wearing everything from workout clothes to super-formal dresses passed us by, some listening to music while others busily talked on their phones. There were also several couples, both young and old, walking their dogs.

In movies, Central Park always looked so empty, like a private garden retreat in the middle of the city. But in real life, it was bustling and crowded, with so much going on underneath the cover of the trees. And it was all still beautiful in its own way.

I snapped a lot of pictures of the people around

us, as well as all the trees, benches, and other features of the park. We eventually stopped at a carousel nestled underneath a white and red brick structure. It was hard to see them at first, but when I went closer, I could see the brightly colored horses. Just seeing all the blues and greens and reds of the horses made me happy. And the fact that there was a carousel in the middle of Central Park made everything feel all the more magical.

I took a picture of the carousel so I could draw it in my sketchbook when I got back to my dorm room.

I was just thinking that we were probably too old to get on the horses when Emma yelled, "I'm going to ride the carousel! Who's with me?"

I whooped, and so did everyone else. Giggling, we paid for our tickets and got onto the carousel. Almost every other kid on the ride was younger than us, and some were so little that their parents had to stand by their horses with them so they wouldn't fall off. A few shrieked and whooped as the horses took us around and around. My friends and I joined in, and we were all hollering, our laughter and voices audible over the loud, cheerful music.

From the ground, Ms. Chang took pictures of us with a big grin on her face.

After we got off the carousel, my friends and I walked around the park some more. In high spirits, we talked and laughed underneath the summer-green trees, wandering around to our hearts' content until our feet hurt.

That was when it hit me. Even though my trip to NYC had not been what I expected, the simple fact that my friends and I were here was a dream come true.

We had made our dream true. Together.

Fourteen

The next few weeks whizzed past us. Christiana continued to pretty much ignore me except to criticize everything I did, and Mr. Hernandez became the unofficial mentor for me, Carolina, and Zeina, giving us tips as we prepared for the showcase. We worked hard to finish as much as we could of our projects, and then somehow it was already the day of the Starscape Showcase.

The showcase was at a gallery near campus. It wasn't until later that night, but we had to set up during the day. Everyone who registered in time got a spot in the exhibition area, which had transparent frames to house each of our works. Since my friends and I signed up at around the same time, most of us managed to reserve gallery spots right next to each other. The only person whose work had to be in a whole other area was Carolina, since she needed a computer set up so people could test-play her game.

I still had a long way to go before I could finish my graphic novel, but I put the first ten pages of it in the display. I'd fully colored and inked everything to make them especially pretty.

The first few pages of Zeina's super-cute cat and dog picture book were on display next to my stuff, and so were Emma's elaborate fashion designs. Sohee's historical Korean graphic novel was also on display, on the other side of Zeina's work.

"Look at us! Displaying our work in an exhibit like

we're professionals!" Carolina cried out with excitement after we'd finished setting up.

"Everything looks so good!" I said. "I'm really proud of us."

"Gather around for a group picture, girls!" Ms. Chang said. "Congratulations on your first exhibit. Here's hoping there will be many more!"

The showcase itself wasn't until later that evening. All my friends—including Sohee—were going to eat dinner together before the event, but since I already had plans with Aunt Yeji and her friend, I was going to have to meet up with them at the showcase.

Technically, the restaurant I was meeting Aunt Yeji at was only a twelve-minute walk from my dorm. But since Mom didn't want me to walk in NYC by myself, she requested a rideshare car for me from all the way back home in Texas.

The ride was only five minutes, but it seemed much longer because my heart was beating so fast for the entire drive. I was so excited to finally see Aunt Yeji and meet her friend Diana. They both seemed so cool!

I arrived ten minutes early, and my mouth fell open as the hostess led me to our table. The restaurant was super fancy, with white tablecloths covering every table. All around me, people were dressed in luxurious gowns and tuxedos. I was wearing what I'd thought was a nice dress for the showcase, but suddenly I felt underdressed.

I opened the menu and gawked at the prices. I couldn't even afford the cheapest appetizer!

Ten minutes passed. Then another ten. When it reached twenty minutes past the time we'd agreed to meet up, I started getting worried.

The server came to check on me.

"Maybe you should try contacting the other members of the party?" he suggested.

"Will do," I said nervously. "Thank you!"

I texted Aunt Yeji.

Hi, Yeji-imo! I'm at the restaurant. Are you and Diana stuck in traffic? Should I go ahead and order for the table?

Five more minutes passed without any response. And then ten more.

The restaurant staff started giving me weird looks. I kept my gaze down, too embarrassed to look up. My stomach growled, and my face was burning hot.

Fifteen more minutes later, Aunt Yeji finally replied.

Gigi, so, so sorry but something came up for work, so I have to catch a flight to Tokyo tonight. I won't be back in the US until the fall, I'm afraid. But how about I visit you in TX the next time I'm stateside? Xx

My entire body went cold as I stared at my phone. I couldn't believe my eyes. Why, and *how* was Aunt Yeji flying to Japan right now?

Barely suppressing the urge to cry, I ran out of the restaurant after a quick "I'm sorry!"

The moment I cleared the doors, I burst into tears. People passing by me did a double take. I was so miserable, I didn't care about being embarrassed anymore. But since it was getting dark, I popped into a nearby coffeehouse, so I wasn't standing in the middle of the busy street.

And then I did the only thing I could think of doing. I called my mom.

"Ji-young?" Mom said when I picked up, calling me by my Korean name. "Are you okay? Did something happen?"

When I explained the situation to her, she let out a big sigh.

"Oh, looks like my sister hasn't changed a bit," she said. "I'm so, so sorry, Gigi. Although I had reservations about you two meeting at first, I really thought she'd be better this time since she'd been doing a good job keeping in contact until now. But I guess I was right to have my suspicions."

I was still sad, but Mom sounded so worried that I said, "It's okay. I have a busy evening planned with my friends. Tonight's the Starscape Showcase, where we're presenting what we worked on during camp."

"That's right. I remember you telling me about that," Mom said, still sounding very concerned. "I'll call Emma's mom to see if she can pick you up and take you to the event. Your friends are already there, right?"

I checked the time on my phone. Somehow, it was already fifteen minutes after the event started! I'd been so sad about everything that had happened with Aunt Yeji that I completely lost track of time.

"Oh, shoot!" I said. "I'm late! And I haven't even eaten dinner."

"Okay, just stay there, Gigi. I will let you know what Ms. Chang says after I call her. Maybe she can get you something to eat, too."

We hung up, and as I waited for Ms. Chang, I realized that although my mom wasn't as cool as Aunt Yeji, she was cool in her own way. Sure, she didn't understand why I loved art so much or why I wanted to become an artist, but she was still always there for me no matter what in ways that no one else ever was.

Because I couldn't express how much I loved her through words at that very moment, I texted her a row of hearts.

Fifteen

Because of really bad traffic, Ms. Chang and I ended up getting to the showcase an hour after the event started. She told me that Emma and the rest of my friends had already presented. Which meant I'd missed my chance to present with my friends like I'd hoped I could.

"You missed all the great questions and applause we got! Everyone was so cool and supportive, too," Carolina said when I arrived. "A few were looking for you after seeing your pages on the display. Maybe they're still around."

My heart felt heavy. I'd worked so hard to present my work at Starscape, only to miss my chance at the very end. But I pressed forward anyway.

"That's okay," I said, trying my best to smile. "At least I'm here now."

I went to stand by my artwork in the hopes that people would stop by and talk to me about my project. A lot of people had already gone home, but some families of the other Starscape students were still around. A handful of professors from the local art colleges were still here too. I kept an eye out for Diana, Aunt Yeji's professor friend, just in case she happened to be here. I'd googled her before today, so I knew what she looked like. But I didn't see her in the crowd.

A few people stopped by my booth to talk to me about my project and read my pages. Carolina was right! Everyone was so nice, complimenting my work and asking questions about my process. None of the other adults said superheroes were overdone, like Christiana said they were. A few professors did say that my line work needed more practice, but they said I had plenty of time to practice more and get better. The adults I enjoyed talking to the most were Mr. Hernandez and his friends, who came by in the last five minutes of the showcase..

"Oh man!" one of the ladies in the group said to me. "These character designs are so creative! And the story sounds so compelling. You should definitely finish this book."

"That's what I've been telling her," Mr. Hernandez said. "Gigi is a really talented artist."

I blushed. "Thank you, Mr. Hernandez. You really helped me improve this month!"

He brought both hands to his chest in a touched gesture. "I'm so glad to hear. Thank *you* for being a great and hardworking student, Gigi."

When the showcase was officially over and it was

just the students and program instructors again, we had the opportunity to visit each other's exhibits. My favorite was Carolina's, because she had a playable game about a cute astronaut frog. It not only boggled my mind that my friend made the game, but I also thought the concept of her game was so cute! I was obviously biased, but it was my favorite out of all the other student games I played while walking around.

The beginning of Zeina's picture book was also amazing, and even just the first few pages made my heart swell up with so many different emotions. It was amazing how much my friend could convey in so few words. Emma's clothes were so cool I could easily picture them making their runway debut in the near future. Last but not least, Sohee's graphic novel was so beautiful and complex already. It was going to be a real masterpiece one day!

Christiana and I may not have seen eye to eye on most things, but we agreed on one: everybody at Starscape was so talented!

Before we went back to our dorms, Ms. Chang and my friends gathered around my display.

"We realized we never got to hear you present your work, Gigi," Zeina said. "So we decided to be the audience for you."

"Yeah, I saw bits and pieces of it, but I'm so excited to hear what you have to say!" added Carolina.

My heart swelled up with joy. I had the best friends.

I looked at Zeina and Carolina, and then at Emma, Sohee, and Ms. Chang. They were all waiting patiently for me to begin.

I was so grateful for their undivided attention, but suddenly, I was also a little nervous. I realized just then that I'd never fully told my friends about my comic book characters before, or the fact that they'd inspired a lot of them.

"Well," I said, clearing my throat. "It's far from being done, but my graphic novel is about a superhero named Metor Girl. In the beginning of the story, she finds herself stranded in the middle of NYC without her powers. But luckily she has awesome friends who help her get them back."

My hands were shaking, and I had to clear my throat again. I glanced at Zeina, who gave me an encouraging smile.

"Her best friend's name is Poetess. She is a powerful enchantress who uses beautiful words to help people and defeat the bad guys." I looked at Carolina, who was giving me a knowing grin. "Then, there is Rocketeer, a genius scientist who saves the world with her high-tech rockets and other cool inventions."

Emma squeezed her fists with excitement when I turned to her.

"The third character's name is Fashionista, who's like Mystique from X-Men but better, because she can not only transform into anyone she wants but can make the most stylish clothes, too."

Finally, I looked at Sohee, who gave me a shy grin.

"Last but not least, there's Virtuosa, who can draw anything she sees and bring it to life. I haven't reached the end of the story yet, but I already know how it's going to end. All hope seems lost for Meteor Girl at the beginning of the story, but she's not only going to regain her powers, but she's also going to save the world, thanks to her friends."

"Gigi, you're so sweet!" Ms. Chang exclaimed.

My friends made sounds of agreement as we all came together in a big hug.

"Yeah, your teacher had no idea what she's talking about," Emma said. "Your story and your art are so great! You should definitely finish it. And let me read it when you're done."

"Same!" Zeina exclaimed.

"Me too!" said Carolina and Sohee.

I nodded, a big smile on my face. "Definitely! I'll send it to you guys when I finish." I thought back to what Emma had said and turned to Sohee. "Speaking of which, have you seen Christiana around? She never came to my display, but maybe she came by when I wasn't here."

Sohee smiled apologetically. "Yeah, she was here

for my presentation. I think she left by the time you arrived, though."

I frowned but tried my best to shrug it off. Oh well. It wasn't like I thought she'd have good things to say about my project, anyway. Looking at everyone's artwork really inspired me to keep drawing and improve as an artist.

When I was back in my dorm room later that night, I filled Paul in over video chat about what had happened with Aunt Yeji.

"Wow, I can't believe she did that," Paul replied. "Sorry, Gigi. I know how much you were looking forward to meeting your aunt and her friend. Who just randomly goes to Japan like that?"

"Yeah, it was weird," I said. I was still sad about what had happened, but I didn't want to dwell on it much right now. I was relieved that I was at least able to have a good showcase with my friends afterward, even though things didn't work out the way I thought they would.

"It's fine," I said. "My mom warned me something like this might happen, and my friends also said I shouldn't trust her, so maybe I shouldn't have been so trusting."

Paul shook his head. "I don't think it's a bad thing to believe in people! And it's definitely not your fault for trusting her. Sometimes some people just let you down, and that's all. It's their problem, not yours."

After we hung up, Sohee asked, "Is everything okay? I couldn't help but overhear what you were talking about with your boyfriend. I was wondering why you got to the showcase so late!"

"Yeah," I said. "Or, at least, it is now."

I explained to her what had happened with my aunt, and Sohee frowned.

"Wow, that stinks. She reminds me of my brother."

"You have a brother who's like that?"

Sohee nodded. "Yup. He goes to Tisch and is still in the city for the summer. My brother is actually the reason why I applied to this summer camp in the first place, even though I don't know anyone else in the US. I wanted to see what his life is like and hopefully hang out with him. But in the end, he wound up being too busy to hang out or do anything together."

I'd been kind of sad about Aunt Yeji, but after hearing about Sohee and her brother, I was even more sad for her. At least I hadn't come to a whole other country for the first time where I didn't know anyone else!

"Wow, I'm so sorry. That really stinks."

"Yeah . . . it was tough at first. But that's why I'm so grateful you invited me to hang out with you and your friends. I'd just have been in my room all day otherwise, since I was too scared to go explore the city on my own."

I smiled. I was so glad Sohee and I were able to help each other feel less alone.

In that moment, I realized that I don't really want to be a famous artist like Aunt Yeji or Christiana. Sure, I wanted to be successful. Who didn't? But I didn't want to do well at the expense of other people's feelings. I wanted to actually value the people around me and make new friends along the way, while also creating art that I really loved and was proud of.

My work was important to me, but so were my friends. And I was going to try my best to keep things that way.

Sixteen

When it was time to move out of our dorm, Sohee and I hugged after we'd finished packing up our stuff.

"You should come visit me in Seoul someday," she said. "Seoul has so many good museums too. You can stay with me and my family at our apartment!"

"That'd be awesome!" I said. "I have family in Korea, but I don't know them well enough to stay with them without my parents."

I decided that should be my next goal. To save money for Korea. Paul had been sending me pictures from his trip, and that'd made me want to visit even more. It'd be so cool to not only have that new experience but also learn more about my own culture!

When my Texas friends and I were all ready to go back home, Ms. Chang called us a car to the airport. During the ride, I looked from one friend to another. Even though we were only gone for a few weeks, everyone looked different somehow. For Carolina and Zeina, the change was subtle, since they were just wearing more chic clothes. Emma, though, looked totally different, since she'd chopped off almost all her hair and cut it into a short bob while we were in the city.

"She wanted to try something new to commemorate the camp," Ms. Chang had explained. "Isn't it very chic and modern?"

I smiled. I loved my mom, but Emma's mom was also really cool.

I wasn't sure whether I looked any different myself, but I definitely *felt* like I changed. I'd learned and experienced a lot in the last month. Christiana never ended up fully accepting the work I did, but I still felt like I learned a lot, thanks to Mr. Hernandez and my friends. My experience at camp wasn't perfect, but it wasn't terrible, either.

"How was Starscape for all of you?" I asked, wondering how the experience was for my friends.

"It was amazing," Carolina said. "I learned so much about video game design, and I definitely want to be a video game designer when I grow up now."

"I feel the same way about making my own kids' books," Zeina said. "What we did at Starscape was so fun!"

"Yeah, I'm definitely moving to New York for college. I love it here," Emma said matter-of-factly. "Although I kind of wish I didn't, because now I'm super doomed."

"Why?" Carolina asked.

"Getting into a school in New York like Columbia or NYU is going to be super hard! I'll actually have to try my best in school! And do all my homework!"

She sighed and we all laughed.

"I don't know about going to college here, but I definitely want to visit the city again too," said Zeina. "We did so much, but I feel like there is still a lot that we didn't get to do."

"Maybe we can save money and come here again," Carolina said. "For fun this time, though. Not to work hard and go to classes like we did this time."

"I'd be down!" I said. "Speaking of saving money, that reminds me. . . . So, about the club . . ."

I trailed off, not wanting to sound too pushy or desperate. We all grew serious as we thought about the fate of the Ace Squad.

"I think I'm pretty burned out," said Zeina. "And I want to have time to do fun things this summer since my parents are probably going to make me go to prep classes to get ready for the next school year."

"And my household—my *life!*—is going to be pretty chaotic for a while," said Carolina. "Thanks to my baby sister. So I don't think I can do club stuff on top of that."

Emma shrugged. "Honestly, I didn't have any good reason for not wanting to do the club again. I could see it being fun if we do continue it, though, so I'm okay with whatever we decide to do."

I looked at each of my friends one by one. I totally understood why Zeina and Carolina didn't want to continue the Ace Squad in the summer. But I didn't want to completely give it up either. Finally, I said, "Okay, then maybe we just take the summer off and restart the club next year? Or at least, reevaluate what we want to do with it then?"

Everyone nodded.

I let out a sigh of relief.

"Yeah," Carolina said. "I think that's a good idea. Worst-case scenario, if we do decide to permanently get rid of the Ace Squad, we should do something else instead."

I perked up. "Like what?"

She shrugged. "Don't know yet, but we can figure everything out later. I liked seeing everyone so regularly this previous school year. I'd hate to not see everyone as much next year."

"I'm afraid of that happening too!" I exclaimed, so glad I hadn't been the only one. "Especially since we have no idea what everyone's schedules will look like for the next school year.

"Maybe we can do something fun," Zeina said. "Like a book club!"

Emma wrinkled her nose. "Or maybe we can just try new places to eat every week or something?"

"I like both ideas!" Carolina replied. "We can vote on it later."

My friends all nodded in agreement.

Even though nothing was decided yet, I felt a lot better knowing that we'd figure everything out together.

Starscape hadn't been what I'd expected it would be, and neither was this summer so far. But after all the fun adventures my friends and I did manage to have, I was excited for what would happen during the rest of the summer and for the school year ahead.

Which Meteor Girl Superheroine Are You?

Grab a piece of paper and writing utensil for this fun personality quiz to figure out which superheroine is the most like you! If your answer to any question is "none of the above," either skip that question or choose the one that sounds the closest to what you would do.

1)   Your ideal day is spent . . .
    a.   Making plans for the future and daydreaming
    b.   Reading (and maybe writing your own!) stories
    c.   Playing video games or learning about space
    d.   Watching movies and TV shows with lots of drama
    e.   Drawing in your room while listening to music

2) **When you see someone in trouble, you . . .**

   a. Cry, but try your best to help anyway

   b. Quickly figure out the best, most peaceful solution

   c. Do mental calculations to figure out the likelihoods of different scenarios, and then act

   d. Yell really loudly and hope there are other people around to help

   e. Might not know what to do to help at that moment, but do whatever you can to make things better later on

3) **In the friend group, you are . . .**

   a. The one with great ideas but not always the best plans to execute them

   b. The one who mediates fights and tries your best to hear both sides of an argument

   c. The one who makes the plans and analyzes their rates of success

   d. The one who makes everyone laugh

   e. The one who is the quietest and shyest but still manages to be a good friend

4) **What are your goals for the future?**

   a. Making your dreams come true and living life to the fullest

   b. Creating stories that help others and make the world a better place

   c. Learning all there is to know about the world and making awesome inventions

   d. Creating awesome runway looks and being featured in a major fashion magazine

   e. Being the best artist you can be

5) If you could change one thing about the world, you would . . .

a. Make it so everyone has enough money to live and make their dreams come true
b. Put more days in the week so you'd have time to read more books
c. Make space travel more affordable and accessible
d. Make it so there are more possibilities for people to express themselves
e. Make it so everyone kept their promises instead of letting each other down

6) When you meet someone for the first time, you . . .

a. Introduce yourself in the friendliest way you can manage
b. Wave and smile while saying hi
c. Quickly learn what their interests are and see if you have any in common
d. Tell them about the coolest thing you did in the past month and ask them about theirs
e. Say nothing and try to figure out if they're friend or foe

7) If you learned that aliens were about to take over the world, you would . . .

a. Hope they're friendly and won't get in the way of you achieving your dreams
b. Quietly observe them at first and find the best way to make peace
c. Already have a plan on how to deal with them, down to what to say when, not if, you make contact
d. Get your supplies ready and prepare to fight
e. Hide in your room and use your phone to check that everyone you know is okay

8) If someone is mean to you, you . . .

   a. Get upset, but do your best to figure out how to overcome it and stay true to yourself
   b. Quietly but firmly tell them that such meanness is not necessary
   c. Respond back with a critique against them
   d. FIGHT
   e. Wonder why this person is even talking to you. Can't they see you have better things to do than listen to their nonsense?

9) Your ideal pet is . . .

   a. Something cute and friendly, like a golden retriever
   b. Something quiet but still fun, like a cat
   c. A robot
   d. Something loud and not afraid to be itself, like a parrot
   e. Something small and adorable, like a rabbit or a chinchilla

10) If you failed to save the world, what would be your downfall?

   a. You lost faith in yourself
   b. You spent too much time trying to avoid conflict
   c. You were so caught up in little details that you lost sight of the big picture
   d. Your emotions got the best of you and you made a careless mistake
   e. You waited too long to ask for help

11) What would you want your legacy to be?

   a. That you did everything in your power to make your dreams come true
   b. That you made the world a better and brighter place
   c. That you advanced technology and thus also the human race
   d. All the "weird" and memorable things you wore and the quotable lines you said
   e. That you did your best with what you could do

12) Finally, which superheroine do *you* think you're most like?

   a. Meteor Girl
   b. Poetess
   c. Rocketeer
   d. Fashionista
   e. Virtuosa

The Results

Read on to see who you're most like! Remember, this is just for fun, and you can be anyone you want to be in the end. We're all so complex; you could also be a combination of multiple people!

Mostly A's: METEOR GIRL

You have big dreams and wear your heart on your sleeve. You love to travel, and your dream superpower is flight and/or teleportation. Not everyone understands you all the time, but that's okay because the ones who matter will. Believe in yourself! You can make your dreams come true. Remember, you can turn to your friends in times of need.

Mostly B's: POETESS

You can be a bit shy, but that doesn't mean you love others any less. You love to read and lose yourself in stories, sometimes preferring fictional characters over real people. You're the peacemaker among your friends and would genuinely wish for world peace if you had the chance. Remember to speak up and let your beautiful words be heard!

Mostly C's: ROCKETEER

People may call you a "geek" or even a mad scientist, but you're not ashamed to pursue your interests and show your true colors. Some people just have ideas, while your inventive spirit, amazing organizational skills, and tenacity make them into reality. You may have a wide range of interests that, combined, make you, you. Why choose between a rocket scientist and a video game designer when you can be both?

Mostly D's: FASHIONISTA

You turn heads, not just because of your impeccable taste but also because of your bold and vibrant personality. You're the loudest person in the room, and so what? Haters are going to hate, anyway. Often the class clown, you make everyone laugh, even in the most serious moments. Keep being you and don't let anyone take away from your shine.

Mostly E's: VIRTUOSA

Even though you may be quiet and shy at first, you stand up for what you believe in and for your friends. People may underestimate or overlook you when they first meet you, but you have incredible hidden talents that make you much more than initially meets the eye. Don't forget to stand up for yourself as much as you do for others.

Don't miss Gigi's first adventure!

Seventh-grade choir is a time to sing for most people, but not for me. I sit in the very back, with my music binder up in front of my face. And when it's not time for me to sing, I draw.

When I put pencil to paper, everything around me fades away except the lines and curves I mark on the page. Even the loud banging of Mr. Martin's piano became muffled as I worked on my latest comic book panel about Meteor Girl, one of my newest characters.

When you live in a quiet and boring suburban town like I do, and your family isn't rich enough to go to cool places like Europe or Colorado like your friends do during breaks, there isn't much else to do to entertain yourself. Drawing is how I have adventures without having to pay a single cent. I may not be able to fly super fast across the night sky as Gigi Shin, but as Meteor Girl, I could fly over the pyramids of Giza and the Eiffel Tower.

"Gigi?" said Mr. Martin, the choir director. "What did I say about drawing in choir?"

I looked up to find myself staring right into the teacher's eyes. Thankfully, he was still behind the piano with both hands on the keyboard—sometimes, when he feels "inspired," he walks up and down the rows—but he looked so mad that I could picture laser beams shooting out of his eyes.

That's when I realized that everyone else in the class was standing up except me. No wonder Mr. Martin could tell I was drawing again.

Oops! I quickly stood and held my choir binder higher up so it was covering my face. A few people behind me snickered, but I didn't look. I was scared of Mr. Martin but not of the other kids in my grade. They already laughed at me plenty last year, when I tried giving myself a chic bob like the ladies in the fashion magazines but gave myself an asymmetrical, crooked haircut that only went to my ears instead. Compared to that, this was nothing.

My hair hadn't fully recovered from that disaster, so I was still wearing a headband now. But it was okay. Headbands were coming back into style. And my red headband with white polka dots was especially cute. It went well with my white silk scarf and red overalls. I managed to get all sorts of cool clothes from the thrift stores in our neighborhood. I loved making my own style!

"Sorry, Mr. Martin," I said. "I'll make sure to pay extra attention for the rest of class."

I snuck a glance at the binder of the girl next to me and saw that we were singing "Do-Re-Mi" from *The Sound of Music*. I flipped to the song. It was easy enough to find since Mr. Martin always printed our sheet music in different colors so we could instantly tell which song was in which packet.

Mr. Martin sighed and shook his head before finally looking away from me. "Okay, class, let's start again from the top of the chorus. *Doe, a deer . . .*"

Like I promised Mr. Martin, I put all my effort into singing, and class went by fast after that. Choir is sort of pointless when you are tone-deaf like me, but it was the only class I could take to fill our school's music requirement. After all, it wasn't like I could draw while holding a violin or a trumpet.

So, even though I hate it, I try to do my best in choir when I'm not drawing.

While I was singing—or trying to sing—I happened to accidentally make eye contact with Paul Kim Wiley, one of the most popular boys in our grade. It was hard not to since the choir chairs formed a U, and as a bass, he was on the exact opposite side of me. When our eyes met, he smiled, and I hid my face with my binder so he couldn't see me blush.

Paul was half white, but he had a Korean mom like me. We had been friends when we were kids since we used to go to the same Korean school, but he stopped going in sixth grade. So we barely talked anymore. He was kinda annoying when we were little, but as a seventh grader, he was cute and nice. All the girls in choir whispered about how he was like a kid K-pop star: great at singing and super polite. He was also on the seventh-grade football team, which made him the closest possible thing to a prince in a Texan school like ours.

When the bell rang, I gathered my things. Next period was art, my all-time favorite. I was so excited that I rushed to the door, not looking where I was going until it was too late.

"Oof!"

I glanced up to see that I'd run smack-dab into Paul. Paul was now a head taller than me, so he had to look down to meet my gaze.

"Oh, sorry, Gigi," he said, even though *I'd* run into *him*.

"It's okay," my mouth replied. I was so nervous that my brain was taking a while to catch up. It was weird how back in Korean school, Paul and I used to mess around and chat effortlessly every week. Now things were so awkward between us, I could barely say two—or three, depending on how you count it—words to him!

"Where are you headed off to?" Paul asked, and it took me a couple of seconds to process what he'd asked.

"Oh, art," I said, almost robotically. "It's my favorite class."

"Oh yeah, I always see you drawing during choir," Paul replied with a smile. "You're really good! I've seen your art on display in the hallway by the art class all the time."

My jaw almost dropped to the floor. "You've looked at my art?"

A funny look crossed over Paul's face, and his cheeks reddened just a bit. "Yeah, one of my friends is also in art, so we meet up together in that area sometimes."

I *had* seen Paul meet up with Caleb, a boy in my class, a couple of times. But I had no idea Paul had even been remotely interested in our artwork.

"Cool," I replied, because that was the only thing I could think of saying. "Well, see you around!"

"See you!" Paul turned and walked away, sounding like he

was as glad as I was that our awkward conversation was over.

If I had any other class next, I would have been too mortified by what had just happened between Paul and me to focus. But sixth period was art, so I pretty much forgot about everything else by the time I stepped into the hallway. Art was the class I share with my best friends, Zeina Hassan and Carolina Garcia. This was the first time the three of us had a class together since fourth grade, so it was awesome.

On my way to the art room, I met up with Zeina, who was coming from English class. Zeina is the first friend I made when I moved to Bluebonnet in kindergarten. We're next-door neighbors, so we grew up making mud pies when we were little and riding our bikes to the library to read manga in fifth grade. She likes to draw, like me, but her main love is reading. She brings a book everywhere, even to art class. Since she also likes to write, she says she wants to make her own picture books one day.

Today Zeina was wearing a sky-blue hijab and had on pretty, robin's-egg-blue flats to match. She usually wasn't as adventurous as I am—which was probably a good thing—but she was still very stylish.

"Your outfit today is so cute!" I said. "I meant to tell you at lunch today but didn't get a chance to comment on it earlier."

Zeina beamed. "Thanks!"

When we walked into the art classroom, there was a big poster on the whiteboard at the front. It had the words "Starscape Young Artists' Program" written in fancy cursive letters and had a picture of a big, fancy brick campus that looked like an Ivy League school. In front of the building were smiling kids painting at easels beneath a grove of willow trees. They looked so happy, like they were having the best time in the world.

Everyone was gathered in front of the poster, chatting excitedly about it. Ms. Williams, the art teacher, was nowhere to be seen. She must have been in the bathroom or something.

Zeina and I walked around the crowd of kids to sit down at the table with our other best friend, Carolina. Carolina had her head down, and I knew she was playing her Nintendo Switch since Ms. Williams wasn't here yet. Carolina loves playing video games and draws cool fan art of her favorite characters. She said she's still deciding on whether she wants to be an astronaut or a video game designer . . . or both! She moved to Bluebonnet at the beginning of fourth grade, and since then the three of us have been as thick as thieves.

"What's that about?" I asked, pointing at the poster.

Without looking up, Carolina replied, "Starscape! It's a prestigious summer art camp on the East Coast. Apparently, they have world-renowned teachers. An artist for one of my favorite video games is teaching this year! And so are famous graphic novelists and other artists."

Zeina and I both perked up. I took my phone out of my pocket and looked up more information about Starscape. Carolina was right. There were a bunch of cool people on the instructor list. I even spotted Christiana Moon, my favorite graphic novelist. I didn't know what I would do if I met Christiana in person, but this was my chance to get advice from the very best. She was Korean American too. Maybe she could help me figure out how to convince my parents to let me pursue art!

The bell rang then, and Ms. Williams rushed into class. Her curly brown hair looked even more frazzled than usual, and her warm dark eyes softened behind her bright red glasses when she saw us all staring at the poster.

"Okay, my artists!" she exclaimed, clapping her hands. "I'm happy to see so many of you excited about this camp, but please get into your seats so we can get started!"

When we all settled down, she continued. "Before we begin today's class, I want to tell everyone about Starscape. It's a summer camp that lasts for a month in one of the most prestigious arts schools in the country. The location changes every year, and this year it'll be hosted by NYU! This will be our seventh year sending kids to this camp. Previous participants later got into many great art colleges, like RISD and Tisch!"

Tisch was my *dream* school, since that's the college Christiana went to. Starscape was also in NYC—and even hosted by NYU this year!—so it seemed like the perfect first step to reach my goal. I really hoped I could get into the camp.

In class later, we were working on our still-life paintings when Ms. Williams came over to inspect our work. She looked at all our artwork with an impressed smile on her face.

"Good job, ladies," she said. "I can always rely on you three to produce amazing work. Are any of you considering applying to Starscape?"

I nodded quickly. "Definitely! I want to go."

Zeina frowned. "I want to go too, but I don't know. I read the poster, and it's super expensive. My parents already pay for my oldest sister's college tuition, and my other sister is going to start next fall."

Ms. Williams winced. "That *is* quite the predicament. Especially since the cost of college is rising so much every year."

Carolina sighed. "My parents probably won't let me go, either. Especially not with the baby on the way. Apparently, babies are expensive. And a lot of work."

Carolina's mom was pregnant with her baby sibling. We

didn't know its gender yet, but we did know they were due sometime next year.

"Congratulations to your mother!" Ms. Williams said. "But, oh dear, yes, this seems like very rough timing all around."

Everyone looked at me, and I stared at the ground.

"My parents don't even know I want to be an artist," I said. "I doubt they'd let me go, even if we could somehow afford it."

Ms. Williams frowned. "Well, that's too bad. On the off chance any of you girls do end up being able to go, be sure to ask me for a teacher recommendation. I'd be more than happy to write glowing letters for all three of you girls!"

"When do we have to apply by?" asked Carolina, scrutinizing the poster at the front of the room.

"Great question, Carolina," Ms. Williams replied. "All the materials are due by December, but it's a rolling admission process, which means that the sooner you apply, the sooner you'll know if you got in or not. You're allowed to submit the artwork you made in class or by yourselves in the last couple of years. If you do decide to create new art to supplement what you've already made, we still have two months until the final deadline."

"And when do we need to have the money by?" Zeina asked.

"Well, aside from the application fee, you don't have to

pay anything unless you get into the program," explained Ms. Williams. "After that, all other fees aren't due until March of next year."

After the teacher left, I turned to my friends. "We *have* to at least try asking our parents. There's no harm in just asking, right? This could really help us in the future if we get in! Even though things may not be ideal now, they might get better by March!"

My friends shrugged. Neither of them looked very hopeful.

"I guess," Zeina replied. "I'll keep you guys updated."

"Same here," Carolina said. "Let's all report back at lunch tomorrow."

"Sounds good." I nodded, clenching my fists in excitement.

My parents probably wouldn't let me go either, but I wanted to remain hopeful. This could be the opportunity of a lifetime!

Acknowledgments

More than for any of my other books, the biggest inspiration for the Gigi Shin series is my friends, especially the ones who have been with me since I was Gigi's age (and sometimes even before that!). Thank you to all my friends, who, throughout the decades, constantly teach me a lot about myself and others. For not giving up on me even in the dark times when I'd given up on myself. You make my world a brighter place.

I would of course also like to thank my agent, Penny Moore, my editor, Alyson Heller, and the other individuals in my team at Simon & Schuster, without whom my middle-grade stories (both the Mindy and Gigi books) would just be ideas in my head. Thank you for trusting me with not one but two different series for kids.

Family plays a lesser role in this book than the previous, but it is a major factor regardless. Just as my friends heavily inspired Gigi's friends, Gigi's mom was greatly inspired by my own. Thank you, Umma, for always being there for me and trying your best to be a good mom, even when we live a whole ocean and a continent away from each other. Like Gigi and her family, my parents and I don't always understand each other, but I'm grateful for our fierce love for one another all the same.

A whole separate thank-you goes to H, who is there for me through thick and thin. Thank you for being my "Paul."

Finally, thank you so much to you, reader, for picking up this book and following along with Gigi's story. I hope you (and everyone else I mentioned in this section, as a matter of fact) never give up on yourself and the pursuit of doing what you love to do. It sounds cliché, I know, but sometimes we all need the reminder. Stay true to yourself like Gigi learned to do in this book. Things may not turn out exactly how we'd like them to, but that doesn't mean great things won't happen. <3

About the Author

LYLA LEE is the bestselling author of YA books about K-pop and K-dramas as well as the Mindy Kim series and the Gigi Shin books for younger readers. Her books have been translated into multiple languages around the world. Originally from South Korea, she's lived in various cities throughout the United States, worked various jobs in Hollywood, and studied psychology and cinematic arts at the University of Southern California. She now lives in Dallas, Texas. Visit Lyla at lylaleebooks.com or on social media @literarylyla.